WON'T KNOW TILL I GET THERE

Steve's parents have decided to adopt Earl Goins, a
thirteen-year-old foster child with a criminal record. Steve
isn't sure it's such a great idea, and just so Earl doesn't
get any ideas, Steve has a plan to show him how tough
he can be. But his plan to spray-paint a subway car
backfires, and lands Steve, Earl and their friends in
juvenile court, where the judge hands down a pretty
stiff sentence: two months working in an old-age home,
with a bunch of feisty, independent senior citizens.

Walter Dean Myers explores some problems of youth
and old age, and the conflicts between them, in this
frank, thoughtful, and funny book.

Charlie Pippin   Candy Dawson Boyd

Chevrolet Saturdays   Candy Dawson Boyd

Fast Sam, Cool Clyde, and Stuff   Walter Dean Myers

Forever Friends   Candy Dawson Boyd

Freedom Songs   Yvette Moore

The Hundred Penny Box   Sharon Bell Mathis

Growin'   Nikki Grimes

Just Like Martin   Ossie Davis

Just My Luck   Emily Moore

Let the Circle Be Unbroken   Mildred D. Taylor

Listen for the Fig Tree   Sharon Bell Mathis

Ludie's Song   Dirlie Herlihy

Marcia   John Steptoe

My Black Me   Arnold Adoff, editor

My Life with Martin Luther King, Jr.   Coretta Scott King

The Road to Memphis   Mildred D. Taylor

Roll of Thunder, Hear My Cry   Mildred D. Taylor

Sidewalk Story   Sharon Bell Mathis

Something to Count On   Emily Moore

Take a Walk in Their Shoes   Glennette Tilley Turner

Teacup Full of Roses   Sharon Bell Mathis

The Young Landlords   Walter Dean Myers

ALSO BY WALTER DEAN MYERS

Fast Sam, Cool Clyde, and Stuff

The Young Landlords

The Nicholas Factor

Motown and Didi

Crystal

WON'T KNOW TILL I GET THERE

WALTER DEAN MYERS

Puffin Books

PUFFIN BOOKS
Published by the Penguin Group
Penguin Putnam Inc., 375 Hudson Street, New York, New York 10014, U.S.A.
Penguin Books Ltd, 27 Wrights Lane, London W8 5TZ, England
Penguin Books Australia Ltd, Ringwood, Victoria, Australia
Penguin Books Canada Ltd, 10 Alcorn Avenue, Toronto, Ontario, Canada M4V 3B2
Penguin Books (N.Z.) Ltd, 182–190 Wairau Road, Auckland 10, New Zealand

Penguin Books Ltd, Registered Offices: Harmondsworth, Middlesex, England

First published in the United States of America by Viking Penguin Inc., 1982
Published in Puffin Books 1988

32 33 34 35 36 37 38 39 40

Library of Congress Cataloging-in-Publication Data
Myers, Walter Dean.   Won't know till I get there.
Reprint. Originally published: New York: Viking Press, 1982.
Summary: Fourteen-year-old Stephen, his new foster brother,
and his friends are sentenced to help out an old age home
for the summer after Stephen is caught writing graffiti on a train.
[1. Old age—Fiction.   2. Foster home care— Fiction]   I. Title.
[PZ7.M992Wo 1988]   [Fic]   87-7340   ISBN 0-14-032612-X

Printed in the United States of America
Set in Caledonia

For Karen, Michael and Chris

for Karen, Michael, and Claire

WON'T KNOW TILL I GET THERE

TO WHOM IT MAY CONCERN: Last year we studied what our English teacher called "personal" writing. Mainly they were diaries and journals, stuff like that. One of the reasons people write that way, she said, is that the writing helps them bring things together, to see where they fit in life. Right now that seems like a good idea. The English teacher said that I write well, and I know I need to get some things together in my own head, so I figured a journal would be cool.

When I thought I was going into coin collecting in a big way (which I didn't), I bought a little fireproof safe. I can keep the journal in there and keep it locked up. Also, I can write it in my father's den. It's his den, but the three of us share it, really. Whoever is in there first has first rights, and the others don't intrude. Usually we don't use it that much. I guess the four of us will be sharing it now. That's more or less what the journal is about—how come there's four of us now.

In the old days they used something like Dear Reader or Dear Diary, but I think I'll just use To Whom It May Concern. No, too long. I'll use initials. TWIMC. Maybe Twimsy. Then if somebody finds it in the year three thousand they can go crazy trying to figure out who Twimsy is.

JUNE 9th   Dear Twimsy:

My name is Stephen Gerard Perry. I am fourteen years old. I was born on Thursday, October 14th, which makes me a Libra. I am also a very nice guy. My grades in school, except for math, were straight B's. I could have done better in math, too, except for the fact that the math teacher didn't like me. Probably something to do with the way I kept failing the math tests.

I live with my parents. My mother's name is Jessica. She works part time for the telephone company. My father's name is Richard; he works for the company that puts out the yearbook for the New York Jets. He decides where the pictures go, what kind of type they're going to use, that kind of thing. Both my parents claim that they love me. My friends say that they like me. That makes me about normal, I figure.

This whole thing started after a few nights of Mom and Dad hanging out in the kitchen and drinking coffee and talking in those low voices they use when they're having a heavy conversation. I remember years ago they went through the same little number. Dad had been working in the post office. Then they called me in one day and said they had decided that Dad was going to quit his job and finish college. So he did. It wasn't any big thing to me, but they were going on like something wonderful had happened. I think they were a little miffed when I said, "So what?"

Okay, so they go through this "deep" conversation bit for a few days, and finally they call me in and tell me to sit down. I figured either Mom was going to quit her job and finish school or I was going to have to quit school and get a job.

Anyway, they start looking at each other and smiling and carrying on, and I could just see that they were really pleased with themselves. Then Mom takes my hand and starts laying it on me.

"Steve, you know we've done fairly well, haven't we?"

"Who?"

"I mean," she said, "we have as a family. We have a nice apartment, a comfortable life, and we get along very well."

"Okay."

"Your father and I were thinking that, although we enjoy sharing these things with you, perhaps we could share them with another child as well."

"Hey, all right," I said. "You gonna have another kid?"

"Not exactly, son." My father started shifting his feet. He always shifted his feet whenever he had more than

3

two words to say. It was like he was warming up. "You see, there are a lot of kids already in the world who don't have the same kinds of things that you have. And we thought we'd like to share our love and our home with one of these kids."

It was definitely getting heavy. They were going to have a kid, but not exactly. The last time I saw somebody not exactly have a kid she had to leave school anyway.

"Well, what do you think?" Mom gave me this little smile.

"I still don't know what you're talking about," I said.

"We're thinking of adopting a child."

"Hey, that's cool."

That really seemed cool. They could go out and adopt a kid and then they wouldn't have to go through all the hassle of having him and everything.

So the next few months went by, and Mom and Dad were going out looking at kids. They'd look at a bunch of kids and then come home and drink a bunch of coffee while they talked about them. It even came to me that they might adopt a girl, but then I figured she wouldn't have any place to sleep.

Then some people came to the house and looked around. They talked to me and asked me a lot of questions that were supposed to check me out but that I wasn't supposed to know were checking me out. Questions like "Are you very afraid when your father finds out that you've done something naughty?"

I've never been afraid when my father catches me wrong, and I told the woman who asked me that I

4

wasn't. She smiled and nodded. She had gray hair, and you just wanted to see her smile and shake that head. She reminded me of that guy on television who sells Sanka.

Then I was told that a kid was coming to live with us. Everybody on the block was excited. That's because I told everybody on the block. I'm not known for keeping my mouth shut. Everybody said it was cool. I have this friend Hi-Note, and he ran down how modern it was and everything. Then, two days before the kid was supposed to show up, I was sitting home checking out my coins (I have this collection of nickels) when a knock came on the door. Little did I know that it was the knock of Unfortunate Destiny.

I got up and answered the door. It was the mailman with a registered letter. He told me to sign for it, and I did.

When the mailman had split, I examined the envelope and saw that it was from the Department of Human Services. I figured it had to be about the new kid. I thought for a while but couldn't figure out what could be in the letter. I decided to make myself some tea while I thought. While holding the letter in my hand and looking at the address to make sure that it was really for my father, some of the steam from the teakettle got on the envelope and loosened up the glue and the letter came open. I took that to be a sign, and so I opened it.

Inside there was a letter saying congratulations on being accepted as a foster parent. It said near the end of the letter that some medical and other reports were included and were to be kept strictly confidential. I looked at the other reports.

Earl Goins was five feet five and a half inches tall, one hundred and twenty-five pounds. There was a list of diseases, and the only one he had had was mumps. Everything else was checked off as normal or satisfactory. I checked his birth date and saw that he was only thirteen, a year younger than me, even though he was an inch and a half taller.

Then I looked at the other report. They gave his addresses over the last five years, and I saw that he had stayed at seven different places. I wondered why, and then I saw the last paragraph. It was the only one not typed, and I had a little trouble reading it. March 1979: disturbing the peace. May 1979: vandalism. October 1979: armed robbery.

The kid was a gangster! My parents had gone out and gotten a gangster to bring into the house!

I put the letter and reports back into the envelope and resealed it. I told myself that I was worrying about nothing. My parents wouldn't bring this guy into the house unless he was reformed or something—or would they?

JUNE 11th He came today. I said I was going out to play ball, and Mom asked me didn't I want to be home to greet Earl when he came.

"No," I said.

She gave Dad a look, and he said something about that being quite all right, and I split.

I went out and there wasn't anybody in the park. I found Hi-Note, and he was on his way to the movie so I went with him.

"When's that guy supposed to come over to your place?" Hi-Note asked.

"He might be there now," I said. "He's supposed to show sometime today."

"How come you ain't home checking him out?"

"I'll see him when I get home," I said. "It ain't no big thing."

"What you gonna call him?" Hi-Note asked.

"Earl," I said. "That's his name."

"That's his real name?"

"Yeah, I saw it on his record," I said.

"You saw his records and everything?"

"Yeah, I did."

"What they say?"

"The same old thing—you know, poor homeless dude ain't got no family, no friends, no place to live," I said. "Got a little record, too, for stealing and whatnot. Lot of kids with no homes get records."

"Yeah, I'm hip," Hi-Note said. "I seen this flick on television where this white cat's parents died, and he ended up with a whole bunch of other kids in a reform school or something, and this dude called Fagin taught him how to steal and everything. At the end of the flick some rich people got him."

"I saw that flick, too. Oliver something, right?"

"Yeah. You see the sequel?"

"They made a sequel to that movie?"

"Yeah, and that's where they showed where he killed the rich people, burned down their house, and put out their kid's eyes and tied him to the radiator down in the basement."

"Get out of here, man."

"What did he do to get a record?" Hi-Note asked. "You can tell me, man."

"Just don't say nothing to him if you see him," I said.

"My lips are sealed. Your secret is safe with me."

"The kid's only thirteen. He did the armed robbery when he was eleven and the other stuff when he was ten."

"Armed robbery? You mean he had a stick?"

"A stick?"

"I got to say stick," Hi-Note said, "because if you tell me the cat had a gun, I'd just go on and have me a heart attack and die before the end-of-the-month rush."

"Say, Hi-Note, why don't you shut up?"

We went to see a Kung Fu movie, and then I walked Hi-Note back to his house. His mother asked me if I wanted to stay for dinner, and I said no, and I went on home.

When I got home, my father was reading the paper, my mother was doing the dishes, and there was a suitcase near the hall closet.

"Hi, Steve, how did your ball game go?" Mom asked. The way she asked, all cheery and bubbly, I figured that the dude must be around somewhere.

"I went to a movie instead," I said.

8

"Earl is in the room," she said.

The room, Twimsy—yesterday it was *my* room. Today it's *the* room. Okay. I went on in to check him out.

Gangster. I took one look at the cat and I knew he was a stone gangster. He was lying out on the bed with a toothpick hanging out of his mouth, looking like he was waiting for somebody to kill. I swear he looked like a bad dream at high noon.

"Hi," I said, extending my hand. "I'm Steve."

"I figured you was," he said.

He didn't move. He didn't stick out his hand. He didn't turn his head. Nothing.

"This is my room," I said. "I'm glad to share it with you."

"Yeah."

"What school you go to?" I asked, sitting on my bed. The bed my parents had bought for Earl was just like mine.

"I don't go to school."

"What do you do?" I asked. "Take a smart pill along with your friendly pill in the morning?"

Earl rolled out of bed slowly and stood up. This was the biggest thirteen-year-old sucker in the world. He looked like King Kong with sneakers.

"What's that supposed to mean?" he asked.

"Nothing," I said.

"Look, let me get one thing straight. I didn't ask to come here. This place ain't no different than any other place I been in, so don't think you're doing me no favor. If you put your mouth on me, I'm gonna bust you up no matter who you think you are."

I didn't say anything else. I lay on the bed for a while,

9

and he went through his things looking for something. He found a toothbrush, and he went out of the room. I got a book and started to look at it. I could only look at the words because my mind was jumping around too much to be doing any reading.

When Earl came back, he put his toothbrush away and lay down again on his bed. I waited for a while and then went out to talk to my father.

"Hey, this guy is something else," I said. "I tried to talk to him, but he acts like I'm stepping on his feet or something."

"Well, son, he's had a hard time," my father answered. "And sometimes when people have a hard time they almost have to deal with that hard time in a way that turns other people off. Give him a chance. He'll come around."

"When? After he cuts my throat when I'm sleeping or something? The guy's been arrested already."

"Did he tell you that?"

"No," I said. "I looked at the letter that came the other day. Maybe I shouldn't have opened it and everything, but that doesn't change the fact that he's been arrested."

"I see where you're coming from," my father said. "You think he should be grateful. Okay, I'll go in and tell him that he doesn't act grateful enough. That just because he doesn't think he's going to be accepted and acts like it, we're not going to accept him. You want me to tell him to get out tonight or can he wait until the morning?"

"That's not fair, Dad," I said. "You're putting the weight on me. I didn't do anything."

10

"I know that, Steve," he said. "Look, son, we feel—your mother and I—that one of the reasons you haven't gotten into the kinds of trouble that Earl has is because we've been fortunate enough to have the kind of home we do. But if this is wrong for you, then it's wrong for us. We thought we'd bring in somebody who needed us more than some of the kids we saw. Maybe the whole idea was wrong."

"Let's see how it works out," I said.

"Is that what you want?"

"I don't know. I guess I want it if it works out."

I went back in the room and read for a while. Earl just stared at the ceiling. I thought of about five cool things to say, but I didn't get any of them out. Then Mom came and said that supper was ready, and we ate.

Earl was polite during supper, but he didn't put himself out to be friendly.

"Perhaps Steve can introduce you to some of his friends tomorrow, Earl," my mother said.

Earl gave a little nod.

"If you play ball you can come to the park with me," I said.

"*If* I play ball?" Earl looked at me as if I'd said something stupid.

That was the last thing he said during supper. My mother was upset—I could tell—but my father looked pleased. After supper Earl went back into the room and closed the door.

"So he thinks he can play ball," my father said. "Maybe, but at least it's something he's got confidence in."

Later on I watched a little television with my parents, and then I went in and sacked out. Earl waited until I got undressed, and then he got into bed. But he didn't put the light out. I got up and put the light out and he asked me what I was doing.

"Putting the light out," I said.

"I don't sleep with the light out," he said. "I got a lot of enemies."

Then he got up and put the light back on.

"I can't sleep with the light on," I said.

"Why you so anxious to get the light out?" he said.

"How about putting a lamp on? That way it won't be so bright that I can't sleep, and you can be looking out for your enemies."

That's how we compromised on our first night together. Sleeping with the lamp on so that King Kong could watch out for his enemies.

JUNE 12th   When I got up in the morning Earl was already up. He was dressed and sitting on the foot of his bed. I looked at him and he looked at me, and he didn't say anything and neither did I. I figured I should try a "good morning" so I did.

Earl grunted.

I go into the kitchen, and Mom's got this big break-fast. The whole works—eggs, pancakes, juice, and home fries. If Earl hadn't been there, I would have gotten the usual—eggs and a lecture.

12

"Good morning." This from Mom.

"Morning." This from me.

Grunt. This from Earl.

Breakfast was cool. Earl said a few words, and his face didn't break or anything, and I didn't get a lecture about what I was going to do with my life.

After breakfast Mom asked what "you boys" were going to do. A broad hint that I was supposed to do something with King Kong. Okay, I figured I'd give it a shot. I told Mom I was going to play a little ball and that Earl could come if he wanted. That pleased her. I finished breakfast about two bites after Earl, dug my basketball out of the closet, and gave Mom a wave.

"Aren't you going to wait for Earl?" she asked.

I looked at him and he said he'd be by later.

I hit the street and it was so hot the tar in the street was getting sticky. My people were on our park bench, talking about how life was treating them wrong and whatnot, and diminishing the world's supply of Gatorade.

My people, by the way, consist chiefly of Hi-Note, who's my Number One Buddy, and this girl named Patty Bramwell. About two years ago we had heard this lecture in school about most people not having even one real friend, so we thought we'd get together and be friends to each other—that way we'd each have at least two friends.

"Hey, I heard you got a hoodlum in your house," Patty said.

I took a look at Hi-Note. It had to be his mouth that went and told everything.

"Look," I said, "he seems to be pretty nice. He just needs a chance."

"I heard that same little speech on the Late Late Show," Hi-Note said. "This couple didn't have no kids, see? And then one night a strange light come into this chick's bed and nine months later she had a kid. Only the kid got this funny look in his eye and acts strange. The chick said he was acting strange and the father—at least he was supposed to be the father—said, 'He's all right, he just needs a chance.'

"First chance the kid got, he wasted everybody in the house and the neighbor's dog."

Patty laughed, but I didn't think it was so funny.

"Look, just don't mention anything about it when you see him. Okay?" I asked.

"If I see the sucker I'm gonna call the police," Patty said.

"Let's play some ball," I suggested.

"Hot as it is?" Hi-Note was taking his sneakers off. "If I even think about any ball on a day like this, I'm liable to have a stroke."

"We were thinking about going down near the river," Patty said, "see if we can catch a breeze."

"Y'all want to go now?" Hi-Note said. "We can pick up some cards and play some Tonk or something."

"Yeah, that's cool," Patty said. "Then about noon we can get some Chicken Delight or something and have a picnic."

"I got to lay for Earl," I said. "He said he might come over to the park."

"This can't be him?" Patty said, looking down the

street. " 'Cause I think I seen this cat's picture on about three different 'Wanted' posters in the post office."

I looked up. It was Earl. He had this small cap that he wore on one side of his head like it was stuck there. But the way he walked was the thing that stuck out most. He walked like he might have had something wrong with his ankle. Every step he took with his right foot was a little dip step.

"Hey, man, you sleep with this cat in the room?" Hi-Note said in a low voice.

"I keep the lights on," I said under my breath as Earl approached.

"Hi, Earl," I said.

He grunted.

"Like you to meet some friends of mine. Hi-Note and Patty."

"Pleased to meet you." This from Patty.

"Heard a lot about you, my man," Hi-Note said. "One thing that wasn't even too bad."

"What's that supposed to mean?" Earl asked.

"Ain't supposed to mean nothing, man," Hi-Note said. "Just one of them sayings."

"Think you better keep your saying to yourself," Earl said.

"Mum's the word, baby." Hi-Note slapped his hand over his mouth. After that friendly exchange we talked about going down to the river again, and Earl said he thought we were going to play ball. I was getting pretty tired of Earl, so I just said we changed our minds. Then we started toward the river.

"Going down to the river" doesn't mean going down

to the river. What we did was go up to Riverside Drive and look down at the river. Then somebody said let's go a little farther. So we did that, just walking and talking. Earl didn't say anything, and I was just as glad that he didn't.

We found a grassy spot and started playing cards. All except Earl, of course. Then he said he was tired of sitting around and wanted to play some ball. I remembered what my father had said, about Earl having confidence in his ball playing, and I figured that if he was really good, he might relax a little and actually even say a few words. I doubted it, but it was worth a try.

Okay, Twimsy, here's where I really blew it.

On the way to the basketball court we had to pass the train yard. The yard was just about empty, and I said we should cut through it to get to the court. It wasn't really much of a shortcut, but I figured that since I was the one who knew about the hole in the fence Earl would be impressed. So we cut through the yards, and Hi-Note is going on about who's got their names written on the sides of the trains and what have you. We're sort of checking out the trains when I saw there was a can of spray paint lying on the ground. I picked it up and shook it, and it was just about full.

I guess I wanted to show Earl I was tough or something, I don't know. The only thing I had ever sprayed in my life was a wastepaper basket, and that was in school for a play.

"What you doing with that?" Patty asked.

I looked at the train and saw that someone had started

16

writing something. The letters "R O Y" were already printed on this old train that they probably hadn't used in a thousand years. The train wasn't even blue, like most of the new trains are—it was brown. So by now I'm feeling kind of cocky, and I know that Earl is wondering about what kind of guy I am. So before I knew it I went over to the train and I added an "A" and an "L" to the "R O Y," making "Royal."

"If I ever get my gang together," I said, "I'm going to call it the Royal Visigoths. The Visigoths were really some tough dudes."

I started adding "Visigoths" and telling everybody about how the Visigoths lived in Spain and how everybody was scared to mess with them and stuff.

"This train is so old they might have ridden it back and forth to their battles," Patty said.

"They rode horses, mostly," I said, trying to remember what I had read about the battles between the Visigoths and the Romans.

Some other guys came up just as I was finishing the "H" in Visigoths. One guy was white and the other black. They were both wearing Pumas. The black guy was wearing shorts, and the white dude was wearing Jordache jeans and wrist bands that matched his sneakers. I figured he was one of those guys who figured if he dressed right it meant he could play ball.

They were older than us but not that much, and I figured they were either going to or headed from the park, too.

"You guys the Visigoths?" the white one asked.

"No. We just writing 'Royal Visigoths' on the train

because we're the Penguins!" Hi-Note gave the cat a look.

"Just asked, man," the other guy said. "I saw your sign on the train before."

"That's so you don't forget us," Patty went on. It didn't take much to get her going. "Whenever you see our sign, you're supposed to take your hat off."

"You know who we are?" the black guy asked.

"We look like mind readers?" I asked, carefully dotting the second "i" in "Visigoths."

"We're the Royal Transit Police," he said, a big smile on his face as he took his badge out of his sneaker.

The two cops took us over to a shack and took our names and addresses. Then they put us in a van and took us over to the juvenile court. I was scared and so was everybody else. Patty started crying, and Hi-Note asked the cops for a break.

"You were the bigmouth!" Patty said. "You were doing all the talking!"

But the cops didn't pay any of us any mind. They were talking about some movie they had seen, like we weren't even there. When we got to court they took our names and addresses again and called our homes. They told Patty's mother to come down and get her. They just checked the rest of our names with the numbers we gave them against the telephone numbers listed in the directory to make sure we weren't lying. Then we were told that they'd let us know when we should come back to court.

Me, Earl, and Hi-Note left. Patty had to wait until her mother came down. I was some kind of glad my mother hadn't been home.

18

I was hoping, Twimsy, that the whole thing was over. I figured we'd get a fine or something like that, and if it wasn't too much we'd just go ahead and pay it. Our parents didn't have to know.

"The only problem with that is Patty," Hi-Note said. "Her mother might start calling around."

"You don't have to worry none about that," Earl said. He hadn't said more than two words the whole time we were being taken to court or anything.

"How come?" I asked.

" 'Cause what they're going to do is either have somebody call your moms or come around and see them. Then when you got to go down to court they got to come with you."

"Both parents?"

"No," Earl said, "but the more people you got down there the easier it is on you."

"They can't do nothing to us, really," Hi-Note said. "All we did was to put a name on the side of a train. That ain't no big deal."

"*You did what?*" Earl stopped and looked at Hi-Note, and Hi-Note took a step back.

"We put a name on a train," Hi-Note said.

"No, man." Earl fished a toothpick out of his pocket and put it in his mouth. "What you did was to Vandalize a Train. You a vandal! Not only that, but you told them you did it to a lot of trains, right?"

"Yeah."

"What I would do if I was you would be to get the rest of your boys to go around and clean off all the other Royal Visigoths signs you got up."

"What boys?" Patty asked.

"The rest of the gang," Earl said.

"What gang?"

"Them Visigoths, man," Earl said.

"I told you when I started writing it that that's what I *would* name a gang *if* I had one."

"So if you don't have a gang called the Visigoths, how come you go around putting the name on all those cars?"

"We don't," Hi-Note said. "We didn't know they were cops so we just made it up."

"You mean I'm in trouble because of what the gang you ain't got didn't do?"

I guess we all are, with a capital "T."

JUNE 19th   Dear Twimsy:

A whole week and nothing's happened. Patty's mother showed up with a lawyer, but when they got there she was just told to go on home and they would call when they wanted her back.

I didn't tell my parents—for one reason. I was chicken. I figured like this—if Earl was right, I'd better tell them so they could come down to court and help me out. But then I also figured like this—maybe they wouldn't find out and I wouldn't get into any trouble.

"Look, man, you better tell your folks," Earl said. "They ain't my folks so it ain't gonna help me, but you should . . ."

"Oh, shut up!" I said. "I didn't get into no trouble before you got here."

20

"You what?"

"You heard what I said." If it hadn't been for trying to impress Earl I wouldn't have been in trouble and I knew it.

"Look, when they get down to court and the judge ask everybody what happened, you know what they're gonna say? They ain't gonna say no 'Hey, there's a new guy here and we did it because of him.' They're gonna say, 'We didn't do it. He's the guilty dude.' And guess who they gonna be pointing to?"

"We were all there," I said.

"Yeah, but you did the dirt!" Earl said. "You the ringleader. They gonna let the girl off easy. They gonna say, 'You go on home and don't do nothing wrong again.' Then they gonna look at you and say, 'Hey, man, we tired of you kids doing this and that, and now we gonna send you to the detention center!' "

Twimsy, things were not looking up.

JUNE 20th   Somebody from Juvenile Court called my father. We were at supper, and as soon as I heard him say Juvenile Court I liked to died. My mother stopped eating and looked at my father. Now, my father is standing at first, and then he sits down on the chair near the telephone and starts shaking his head and looking like the whole world just fell on him, and I know the end is near. He wrote down some dates and then hung up the phone.

"Can I see you in the bedroom, Jessica?" he says.

When they split, I looked over at Earl, and he was greasing away on a chicken thigh.

"How come you can eat at a time like this?" I asked.

"If you knew how the food is in Juvenile Hall," he said, sucking the last piece of meat from the bone, "you'd be eating as much as you could, too."

For a wild moment I figured maybe it wasn't about me, maybe it was just something about Earl. Then I heard my mother crying. I reached for another piece of chicken.

My father came in and told us what the call had been about. He asked us if it was true, and we both said yes.

"Why?" my mother asked.

Twimsy, I hated to see the way she looked, crying and everything. The thing was that I didn't see where we had done anything *that* bad. I mean, I knew it was wrong, but it wasn't as if we had mugged somebody or something. I guess it was the idea of the court calling and everything that made it seem so bad.

Trying to explain to my father that I was the only one that did it didn't help, either. And if painting the name of a gang that you didn't have on a train sounded stupid the first time you explained it, the second time seemed ridiculous altogether. And I couldn't say that because Earl was kind of tough I wanted to be tough, too. I just couldn't say that.

JUNE 24th Twimsy, there must have been a thousand kids in Juvenile Court when we got there. Some of their parents were there, some weren't. A clerk would come out and call out your name and tell you what room to go into. We got there at eight-thirty and our case wasn't called until nearly three o'clock in the afternoon. I tried to see how everybody else was doing, and they seemed to be doing okay, mostly. Least they weren't going to jail. Most of the kids got probation, and that's what I figured we'd get. Patty's parents had their lawyer and were off to one side. My parents were sitting real quiet, and I could see that they were messed around. It was as if I had really done something terrible, which I didn't feel I had. I didn't steal anything or hurt anybody, and I was willing to go clean the car off if that's what they wanted. But I think it was the idea of them having to come down to court and figuring what people would say and everything. My father hadn't spoken much in the week since he got the phone call, and I wasn't anxious to talk to him.

At two-thirty three guys came out, and there were guards with them. They were being sent to a juvenile detention center. They came out and said good-bye to their friends and everything while they were waiting for transportation to the center. Hi-Note asked one of them what they did, and they said they had put toilet tissue in a pay phone so the money would stick up there. When they went back to get it, the cops got them. When my mother heard that, she started crying again.

"Hey, man, what you here for?" This guy comes over to where me and Earl are sitting. The guy's wearing a

T-shirt that says, "I Hate Me So You Know What I Think About You."

I said vandalizing a train, but I said it kind of under my breath so my moms wouldn't get into crying again, which she did whenever she heard the word.

"That's what you done, huh?" the guy says. "Well, they made a mistake on me. I'm innocent. I was running down the street and trying to see how fast I could go . . . you know what I mean?"

"Yeah."

"So I was running and I had my head down, like this . . ."

He got into a running position with his head down and his arms swinging.

"You can't see where you be going when you got your head down like that, right?"

"Yeah."

"What you mean, yeah?"

"I mean right," I said.

"Yeah. So I accidentally hooks this lady's pocketbook, see—did I tell you about how fast I was going?"

"Yeah."

"So I look up and I see this pocketbook on my arm— you know what I mean?"

"Yeah?"

"I must have hooked it when I ran by her, see, only by this time I'm around the corner and I don't know where it came from. I looked around and I don't see nobody, so I figured I'd better check out whose it is, you know what I mean?"

"Yeah."

"That's Good Samaritan stuff. Anyway, then this cop come around the corner yelling stop and stuff like that, and I ask him was it his bag. You know, you got all kinds of cops on the force now, if you *really* know what I mean."

"Yeah."

"Fool locked me up, said I snatched the lady's purse."

"No!"

"Yeah, he did! Locked me up like I was a thief!"

"Yeah, but you just tell 'em that story," I said. "I'm sure they're going to understand."

"I don't know, man," he said, shaking his head. "They used to have this judge named Joe, and they called him, 'Let-'Em-Go Joe.' You had a chance with him. Now they got one named Jim and they call him 'Stick-'Em-In Jim.' I sure hope I don't get him. They say he ain't got no understanding at *all*. You know what I mean?"

I said yeah one more time and hoped I didn't get him either.

At three o'clock, almost on the nose, they called us. When we were just about ready to go in, my father spoke to me.

"Son, whatever happens," he said, and there were tears in his eyes, "your mother and I love you and we'll support you."

I really wish he hadn't said that because it really made the whole thing seem super serious.

We went into a small room and there was a lady dressed in black robes sitting at a table. She was kind of small and black, and I felt good about that. We sat down and she read some papers. Then she looked up at us and took her glasses off and asked us all to stand when she called our names and say if we were guilty of painting the train or not.

"Your Honor." It was Patty's lawyer, a tall thin Puerto Rican guy. "It is my understanding that only one of the young people actually participated in the act of vandalism."

"They presented themselves as a group, a gang," the judge said. "Whether they are actually a gang or not is immaterial. They entered Transit Authority property as a group, they participated in the action as a group."

Then she called the names and we all stood and said that we were guilty. Patty said it so low you could hardly hear her, and the judge made her repeat it. I could see that her being black wasn't going to help.

"Are there any mitigating circumstances this court should be aware of before a sentence is passed?" the judge asked.

First Patty's lawyer stood up and said how nice Patty was and that she had never been in trouble.

Then the parents got up, one set at a time, and spoke for the rest of us. While they were talking, I remembered one guy who had been accused of robbing little kids in the school and who had gotten probation, so I figured we'd get probation. The only ones I saw going to the detention hall were the guys with the telephone thing, and I figured that maybe they had records or something.

My father spoke for me and Earl, saying how we were good kids and that kind of thing, and please could we have another chance. When everyone was finished, the judge looked through the papers, which I figured must have been the information the people who called the houses got. Then she took off her glasses again and spoke to us.

"It's bad enough when children who have a history of trouble continue to get into trouble," she said. "That is a loss both to the community and to the society at large. However, it's a far greater loss when children who have had no difficulties—so-called good children—assume that mindless vandalism is something that society will tolerate. In my mind the loss to society is far greater, for these are the people we are depending on to lead us on into the future. And the only way they can lead us is to assume the responsibilities that are typical of members of a thriving community.

"My first impulse is to have these young people spend some time in a place for wayward youth, so that if they don't know what is expected of them, or don't think that it's important, they will have the chance to reflect on their options in the harsher light. I don't think that two or three months in this kind of detention home would be too harsh, and I think it far superior to a fine.

"However, another situation has arisen in the community in which most of you live, which presents, I think, a unique learning opportunity. A community home for senior citizens which is scheduled to be closed at the end of the summer has a dire need for additional help. Therefore, I am giving all of you young people a choice. You can serve the two months' penalty time I am imposing on you in a detention home, or you can serve it by working in the senior citizens' center that happens to be in the community in which you live. If you decide to serve in the community center, then you can live at home and report to the center each morning at eight o'clock, six days a week, for the duration of June, all of July, and the first three weeks of August, or you can report Monday morning to the detention center. What is your choice?"

Choice? What choice?

JUNE 25th   Dear Twimsy:

So far, so good. Just got home from the Micheaux House for Senior Citizens. The first day was a breeze. We got there and we met this lady named June Davenport. She runs the place and seems, more or less, okay. She told us that the city was going to close Micheaux House because it was more efficient to run larger places than it was to run a place like Micheaux with only twenty residents. (Right now there are only six residents.) The trouble, though, was that most of the help had been transferred to the new place.

Micheaux House was a three-story red brick building that had been converted from a really nice town house to an apartment building and then to a home for senior citizens. There were carved figures over the front entrance which were repeated in a smaller version over the windows of the top story. It seemed to squat right in the middle of the block, slightly higher than the brownstones on either side of it, thinking of itself as slightly better than the rest. It gave you the feeling that if it had been human it would have been a fat old man who used to have a lot of money.

The first floor consisted of two small offices, a first-aid room, and a large hall. The second floor had a good-sized recreation room and some kitchenette-type apartments. There were more rooms on the third floor, but they didn't have kitchens, although there was one room that was just a place to cook and store food. There was a small library on the third floor, too.

A guy named London Brown did the maintenance work and doubled as a kind of male nurse.

The funny thing was that I had seen Micheaux House for years but really hadn't paid any attention to it. I couldn't ever remember any of my friends going in or out of there, or even having seen anybody just hanging around the place. But dig it, Twimsy, I never really notice old people anyway. I mean, I look at them but I don't see them. I guess you have to have people on your mind to take notice of them.

JUNE 29th   It's easier to deal with the way my moms acts than the way Dad does his thing. Moms was hurt, and that made me feel bad. But Dad hasn't gotten off the kick about why I did it. He wants me to give him a reason even when I've told him I can't. That's the way he usually is. You do something stupid or because you weren't thinking, and he asks you to give him a reason, and so you just sit around and feel stupid until he forgets about it. But I don't like it when Earl is around.

There was a lecture, too. It lasted right through "Those Amazing Animals" and halfway through a special. Then both Earl and I were told to go to our room and think about what my father had said.

"He was saying we were lucky we didn't have to go to the detention hall," I said as I watched Earl relace his sneakers. He had about five different ways he could lace his sneakers, and when he didn't have anything else to do, he'd take the strings out and relace them. It was like a nervous habit. "But I don't think that judge really was thinking about sending us there. She probably just wanted to get us to work in Micheaux House."

"If that had been me by myself, she'd have busted my tail," Earl said. "I'd be in the slam right now."

"I don't think so," I said.

"What do you know?" he said. "Anybody who collects money just to look at don't know nothing about no real life."

"What you mean by that?" I asked.

"I see you messing with them nickels," he said. "I see you."

Twimsy, the way he said that it was like I was doing something freaky and he had caught me. And the thing was, he was saying that I was doing something strange because I collected nickels, and I thought that he was a little strange to think there was anything wrong with collecting coins. I was always taught that people were basically just the same. I'm beginning to wonder about Earl.

JUNE 30th Dear Twimsy:

We hardly see any of the old people. We just sit around and play checkers or pool all day. Earl is about the best pool player I've ever seen. He never shoots the ball hard or anything like that. He just kind of *eases* the balls into the pockets. We also played Ping-Pong with him, but nobody was nearly as good as he is. I asked him how come he could play Ping-Pong and pool like that, and in his usual nasty way he just said, "Guess."

Anyway, Twimsy, that's not the big news. The big news is that Hi-Note came this close to getting himself killed.

We were signing in (which we have to do every morning) and watching London Brown stuff himself with a hero. This man can kill a hero like *nobody* can.

In the first place London weighs over three hundred pounds. He's really huge. He gets these hero sandwiches and eats them from the end. If you can imagine a submarine drifting into Fu Manchu's Cave of Death, you can just about imagine how London looks eating a hero sandwich. After every bite there's little pieces of onion and tomato hanging out the side of his mouth and juice running down his chin. If the Moral Majority ever dug this dude eating a hero, they'd rate him X and ban him from life.

Anyway, Patty was the first to sign in, and she went upstairs. The rest of us had just finished signing in when down comes Patty and tells us that the old people were sitting in the recreation room. Naturally we went right up there to check them out.

They were sitting around in chairs just talking real quiet between themselves. But what they were really doing was checking *us* out. Now, Miss Davenport had told us that we were there to assist the senior citizens if they asked us to, and said not to mess with them if they didn't ask. But after a while, with them sitting around whispering to each other and peeping at us and us sitting around peeping at them, something had to give. So when one of the women coughed a little, Hi-Note jumped up and got her a glass of water. She said she didn't want any water.

"Hey, I'm just trying to be cool," Hi-Note said. "You coughed so you must need some water."

"No, thank you," the woman said. She was a small-lish, brown-skinned woman with big dark eyes.

"It ain't poison!" Hi-Note said.

"The lady said she doesn't want your water!" One of the old guys stood up. He was thin, with legs that looked a little too short for his body. He had a big nose and a large mustache that was mostly gray.

"I didn't say anything to you," Hi-Note said. "So why don't you just cool out."

"I spoke to you!" the old guy said.

I could see that the old guy was getting pissed and it was funny. Hi-Note could probably blow this guy away with one puff.

"Forget him," another of the old guys said. "Let's go play some cards."

"Yeah, you'd better go on and do that."

"You can cool it too, Hi-Note," Patty said.

"High Boat? What kind of a name is that?" the man with the mustache asked.

"Hi-Note!" Hi-Note said. "You'd better turn your hearing aid back up."

"Hi-Note? That's a name for a boy?"

"Get off my name, man," Hi-Note said.

"What's the matter, your mother didn't like what she saw to give you a name like that?"

"That's not my name," Hi-Note said. "It's just what people call me. Why don't you just leave it alone?"

"When your voice changes, are they going to call you Low-Note?" the guy asked.

Everybody cracked up, but Hi-Note was getting hot under the collar. So then he made his mistake. He went over to the guy and just stood next to him so the guy could see he wasn't afraid.

"You threaten me?" Mustache turned deep red. "You threaten me? I challenge you to a duel!"

"Dry up and blow away, old man," Hi-Note said.

"You are afraid of my challenge? You don't accept?"

"Yeah, I accept," Hi-Note was looking down at the dude.

Then the old man just turned and walked out of the room and we thought it was over. Patty was laughing the hardest, and Hi-Note was shaking his head. None of the old people were laughing. Earl just kept on shooting pool. The old man came back with two canes and told Hi-Note to take one.

Hi-Note smiled and took one of the canes.

"Don't get into anything," Patty said to Hi-Note. "This kind of thing gets started and before you know it somebody gets hurt."

"We're going to sword-fight with these, right?" Hi-Note smiled some more and got into his sword-fighting stance.

"Precisely!" the old man said. Then he held the bottom of the cane and pulled out the handle.

It was one of those sword canes. That shut everybody up. Hi-Note gave his a little pull, and there was a sword there, too.

"My name is Pietro Santini, Mr. Hi-Note," the man said. "I just want you to know who it is that kills you this morning." He was very serious.

"Hey, look, man, I don't want to hurt you, dig?" Hi-Note said. "So why don't you just put these toys up and go back to your nap or something."

Pietro Santini walked toward Hi-Note and with a flick of his wrist took a button off Hi-Note's shirt with the sword. I stood up as Hi-Note went to lift the sword he had in his hand. But before he could raise it to his belt, Santini had knocked it out of his hand.

"You may pick it up," he said. "If you have the nerve."

Hi-Note looked over at me, and I shook my head no.

I think Hi-Note was just about ready to sit down when Earl spoke up.

34

"I don't think he's got the nerve to pick it up," he said nastily.

Hi-Note went over to the sword and picked it up carefully and turned toward Santini. Santini came to him quickly and tapped him on the top of his sneaker with his sword and then took another button off his shirt. It was a good thing it was one of those very loose shirts. I could see that Hi-Note wanted to walk away and forget the whole thing.

"Hey, Hi-Note, you scared?" Earl again.

"Hey, Earl, why don't you shut up?" I said.

"Why don't you come over here and shut me up?" he said. He made a shot, and I watched as the cue ball hit the one, sent it into the cushion and then across the table into the side pocket.

Santini came toward Hi-Note again, and Hi-Note backed against the wall. Santini then hit the wall next to his shoulder and knocked the sword out of his hand.

"Well?" Santini asked, waving the sword a few inches in front of Hi-Note's face.

"Hey, man, I'm sorry," Hi-Note said. "I didn't mean anything. . . ."

"How could you?" Santini asked. "You don't know anything."

"That's right," Hi-Note said, staring at the point of the sword. "I was thinking the same thing myself."

Santini put away his sword and picked up the other one. Then, taking the woman Hi-Note had been talking to by the arm, he left the recreation room. The others left with them. You could just see they were happy as anything.

"Who is that cat anyway?" Hi-Note asked. "Count

of Monte Cristo or somebody?"

"You want me to go get him so you can ask him?"
Patty asked.

"Hey, Earl, you almost got me killed," Hi-Note said.
"How come you had to put your two cents in it?"

"If the old cat did your butt in, it would be something to talk about," Earl said, smiling. "I mean, what
can you say about a game of pool?"

"You people can laugh," Hi-Note said, "but I was the
one that got chumped off."

Hi-Note took a magazine from the rack and sat in the
corner by himself. He's got this really pointy kind of
nose, and when he gets mad he holds his head so that
it looks like he's pointing up with his nose. When he
sat down with the magazine, the nose was pointing to
about twelve o'clock. I thought about calling him Hi-
Nose, but I didn't think he was in the mood for any
jokes.

Later in the day a couple of the old folks—the black
woman named Mabel Jackson and the tall thin white
woman—came out together and got some magazines and
took them back to their rooms or wherever they go
when they're not in the recreation room. We're not
allowed to go into their rooms unless we're invited or
assigned to do something. When they came out, it
dawned on me that it was the first time that I had seen
any of them come out naturally. Usually they would
come as a group, or if you saw one or two they would
be looking around. But these two just came out together very casually. It came to me that they were

probably afraid of us and that Santini was doing his thing to show us that he was just as tough as we were or something like that. It would have been easier with a can of spray paint, and safer, too.

JULY 2nd   Dear Twimsy:

Today Earl got into a tussle with London Brown. No one really tells us what to do at Micheaux House. The old people don't really rap to us unless they have to, and Miss Davenport isn't there half the time. She told Patty that she didn't have to be there at all, that she had been assigned to a new place, but she had worked at Micheaux House for a long time and felt something special for the old people and the place. Anyway, every once in a while London Brown will tell us to do something and we'll do it. Mostly dusting or picking up something that we left lying around, 'cause the old people are pretty neat. But every once in a while he gets a real attitude and starts bossing us around. Today he did that, and I think Earl was just the closest to him. Earl wasn't so much sweeping as he was pushing the dirt along the edge of the rug.

"You mean you don't know how to sweep a floor?" London snatched the broom from Earl. "You sweep like this!"

London swept real hard for about five feet, and then he threw the broom toward Earl. He could have been throwing to him, which I thought he was, or at him, which Earl must have thought, because Earl hit London like I never seen anyone hit. London stumbled back about two steps and shook his head.

The only old person in the room at the time was Mabel Jackson. Mabel was black and in her seventies.

"Shame on you!" she called out as she went over to London Brown. "Just shame on you!"

I figured London Brown, as big as he was, could have wasted Earl easily. But he just looked at him, felt his jaw, and walked away. He stopped at the door and turned toward Earl again, as if he was still making up his mind about what he would do, but then he just left.

"Shame on you!" Mabel Jackson's fists were clenched, and the vein that stood out in her neck moved as she spit out the words at Earl. "Ain't you got no decency in you? Shame on you!"

Then she walked out. The room was dead still. The only thing that seemed to be alive in the room at that time was the words that Mabel Jackson had left. I felt bad about what Earl had done, and I felt a little sorry for him, too.

JULY 3rd   Dear Twimsy:

Things were bad between us and the old people after that. No one was saying much of anything when Patty came up with an idea. She said, "Let's have a Picture Day."

Now I didn't think much of this, and at first the old people didn't respond at all. Then one of them, Eileen, said that she thought it might be a good idea and that we could all bring in pictures the next day. I think she knew that things were tense and just wanted to ease them out a little. So it was agreed, tomorrow we bring in the pictures.

But for the rest of the day we sat around doing nothing, hardly even talking. Some of the guys from the block came around last night and asked me if I wanted to play on a softball team. Sam Jones, the guy who plays on the University of Arizona team, is home for the summer, and he was looking for a team to play in an all-city softball league. You know, Twimsy, if anybody asks me what I want to be, I tell them I want to teach, but that's not really true. My number-one thing is playing baseball, but when you tell people that they think you're being unrealistic.

I would also like to be a writer, but when I say that, they ask me what I'm going to write about, and then I have to say I don't know, and that opens the door to a lot of funny looks.

Anyway, no baseball or softball this summer. It doesn't even seem hot. It is hot out, but I'm parked in Micheaux House all day in the air conditioning, and I can't even enjoy the sun.

Another thing I don't have any more is privacy. I thought I'd share a room with Earl. That sounded okay. But that's not what happened. What happened is that I had a place I could go to and be alone or do anything I wanted to—now I don't. If I didn't feel like talking to anybody, I'd just go in my room and shut the door.

That's gone. What I lost was privacy, and what I'm sharing is just a room. I think I'll stop writing before I really get myself depressed.

JULY 4th Picture Day!!!   The pictures were dynamite. I've never seen so many pictures in my entire life. I didn't expect the old people to get so involved with Picture Day but they did. It was a little strange, really. The day before, they were really kind of standoffish, but on Picture Day they seemed anxious to show us what they had brought in. I'm going to run down what each person brought.

Me:

I brought in pictures of me when I was in elementary school and when I was with my parents at Jones Beach. I also brought in one picture of me with my Little League team.

Patty:

She must have had more pictures than anyone else in the world, but they were all the same, or just about the same. It's always a picture of Patty standing next to somebody with this big smile on her face and her arms folded. She's always right in the center of the picture, too.

Hi-Note:

He brought in a picture of him dunking a basketball.

40

I was with him at the time, and I know he was really standing on a ladder when the picture was being taken.

London:

No pictures. He went on about how he didn't think we really meant it and stuff like that when he knew we did. Sometimes I think London is a little strange. As a matter of fact, sometimes I think everybody is a little strange—except me, of course.

Pietro Santini:

Santini is thin and his back is just a little round—not a lot, just a little. That makes him look a little mild-mannered. In his pictures, though, he looked like the kind of guy you wouldn't try anything with. Two of the pictures that he had were of him behind the counter of his grocery store. Another one was of him in a bathing suit at Coney Island. It was one of those old-time bathing suits that looked like striped underwear, and Santini laughed at it more than anybody. But the most impressive picture of Santini was one of him all dressed up in a big coat with his foot on the fender of a car. His hair, which is now gray, was dark and curly, and he wore a thin mustache that made him look like an old movie star.

In all of Santini's pictures he was by himself. Even the one at Coney Island had the water in the background and no other people.

Mabel Jackson:

Mabel Jackson's pictures were a little bit of a shock. She's a very pleasant-looking woman, about medium

41

brown, and a little lumpy in the body. She brought in these pictures that were taken in front of her church. In one she was standing next to the pastor. She had on this enormous hat, and she was wearing white gloves. But what was so surprising was that she looked a lot like Patty. She really did. Another picture was with a girl that she said was her cousin. In Mabel Jackson's pictures she stood a little back from the person she was with and looked at them.

Esther Cruz:

Esther Cruz is really short and looks very friendly. If you see her in the hall or something, she'll smile every time. She's almost the same color as Mabel Jackson, but in her pictures she looked lighter. The two pictures she brought were both with her son. In one she was standing in front of an apartment house she said had been torn down and projects built in its place. The other picture was of her and her son in front of a Christmas tree. Her son was in his pajamas opening presents, and he was a little blurred, as if he had moved just as the picture was being taken. There was a television set in the background with a round picture tube.

Jack Lasher:

Jack Lasher never smiled, or at least I've never seen him smile, and he wasn't smiling in his picture. He had only one picture—it was of himself and three of his friends. They were in uniform and had rifles and helmets, standing outside of a small place that could have been a grass hut or grass and mud—I couldn't tell. They had their arms around each other. The picture was yellow, and one corner was faded more than the rest. He pointed to each of the other guys in the picture—they must have been nineteen or twenty—and told where each of them had died.

Two had been killed at the very place where the picture had been taken, Bataan, and another had been killed on an island whose name he couldn't remember. Patty asked him was he very close to those guys, and he gave her a funny answer. He said that he hadn't really been close to them while they were alive but had drawn closer when they were killed.

Twimsy, when he said this his voice broke and he turned away. Jack Lasher's a big, strong man. I guess he's always been big. In the picture he had his sleeves rolled up, and you could see that his arms were large. He was taller than the guys who died, too.

Eileen Lardner:

Eileen Lardner wasn't the prettiest person in the world, and never had been. You could tell that, even though, like most old people, she had kind of mellowed out in her looks. But while she was tall and a little graceful now, in her pictures she was tall and just plain skinny. She was dressed in a nurse's uniform in one and in these really long skirts in the other two. The other two pictures were of her holding a cat in her lap. She had her head tilted slightly downward and looked up with her eyes. She does that a lot now, so I guess she hasn't changed much.

Twimsy, all in all the picture session was one of the most interesting things that has happened at Micheaux House. When I think about the old people, I think about them in a modern setting, but when I saw the pictures, many of them old and faded, it gave them completely different lives as far as I was concerned. It was as if they had lived before, when they were young, and were living again now, during the time that I was young. I think this might be the wrong way to think about them. Maybe I should be thinking about them as just living one life. What I am doing, I think, is something like what Mabel said the other day. I thought the present belonged to me and that they weren't a part of it.

Also, although none of the old people looked at each other's pictures very much, they were really anxious to make sure that me, Patty, Hi-Note, and Earl saw their pictures. I got the feeling that they wanted to make sure that we knew that they had been young once.

JULY 5th   A guy from the neighborhood came over to Micheaux House today. He brought this pile of old magazines, all tied with a string, and asked me if they had a magazine rack. I showed him where it was, and he took the magazines over to the rack and starting putting them in. Then about halfway through he stopped.

"I didn't know they got all the latest magazines," he said.

Then he split. Just like that. He was acting like he was disappointed or something.

"What he do, bring some old magazines?" Mabel Jackson asked.

"Yeah," I said, "then he got mad about something and split."

"Lot of people do that," she said. "They sit home and think about what some old people might want and then they bring it. We had a lady who was visiting us from someplace—oh, yes, Kansas. Young thing she was, studying about how to take care of senior citizens at some school. She brought us these blankets. They were nice, but we didn't need any blankets. We got plenty of blankets. It don't mean nothing, though. Girl's heart was in the right place."

"How come you stay here?" I asked.

"How come you asking?" She had this really nice smile that made you smile along with her.

"Just asking."

"Well, you reach a certain age, and you look around at your life, and you figure out what's best for you," she said. She was making this large quilt with a star pattern. "I reached that age and started looking around and I seed that I wasn't what you would call no spring chicken. I was getting scared of the children. Children don't mean to hurt you—they just don't take you seriously. You see a bunch of young boys running down the street, you know they busy being young boys and ain't paying not a bit of mind to you shuffling along. You lose your strength, you get scared easy.

"Then there's the mean ones. People looking to hurt you 'cause they think you got a few pennies. I found

45

myself staying home more and more. Sitting in my kitchen thinking about what I used to do. I said to myself, 'Child, you better get on up from there and do something with yourself.' I looked around and seed this place. This is an old place, been around for a long time. People here from when this place wasn't Harlem. See, this whole section used to be just the edge of Harlem. That's why you still got white folks and everything else around here. I come in here once or twice when they used to hold what they called senior socials, and I liked it. Then I just moved on in. I got people to talk with, argue with, a few little things to do. It's okay, you know."

"And those quilts," I said.

"This thing?" Mabel Jackson held the quilt up. "This ain't nothing to what we used to do down in Atlanta and around Valdosta. But it's something to do, ain't it?"

JULY 6th   So it's Sunday morning and I get up and I'm feeling pretty good. Earl's still sleeping. We were up late last night watching an old movie about Frankenstein. This was the first time I really dug Frankenstein's monster. (Also the first time I realized the guy they created wasn't named Frankenstein.) Anyway, we had a pizza, and the pizza box was on the floor, and so were the outside crusts, which Earl doesn't eat but which I do, and also some empty soda cans. Big night. The room looks like it just went through some kind of shock test.

Then, to top it all off, I'm lying there, trying to figure out whether some paint cracks on the ceiling look like a guy or a map, when Earl wakes up and throws his pillow at me. Nothing hard, just kind of lobs it over. Now, I've been doing this to him sometimes because he always sleeps late and when he has to get to Micheaux House by eight-thirty. I don't want to shake him, so I just kind of lob a pillow at him and he wakes right up. But this is Sunday, so I know he's just fooling around. I lob the pillow back and follow it up with my own pillow. Before you know it the pillows are flying back and forth. Wham! Wham!

In comes my father and says that Mom doesn't feel well and isn't going to church. He says we should clean the room up and come and have breakfast, and then we'll go, the three of us, to church. That's cool.

Only Earl doesn't help with the cleaning. I start gathering things up from the floor, including his stinky behind sneakers, and he's just lying there.

"You waiting for a formal invitation to the party?" I ask.

"Why don't you cool out?" he says.

Okay, that aggravates me from jump street. Every time he's supposed to do something and I tell him, he looks at me like I'm some kind of nut and asks me how come I don't cool out. So if he's not going to clean up half the room, I'm not cleaning up half. As I said, he doesn't eat the crusts and I do, but his crusts are all over the floor, especially after the pillow fight. Everything is all over everything. I wash and come out to the kitchen, he washes and comes out to the kitchen, and we have breakfast. Mom doesn't look so good. What she's got is a summer cold, and she really looks like she's miserable, and I feel kind of sorry for her. We have breakfast and then the three of us—me, Earl, and Dad—go off to church.

Dad enjoys having us go to church with him. You can take a look at him and tell he's getting off on it. Okay, so lately I've been feeling cooler with this kind of thing. He's proud of me—or of us, when Earl is around—and that's good. I guess it's a way of feeling for somebody. I know I like to talk to my friends about his job a little—it makes me feel good. So I sit up in church and say hello to everybody I'm supposed to say hello to, and Earl grunts every once in a while. I think if he died and took the wrong bus and ended up in heaven and God met him at the gates, he'd just grunt and try to bop on in.

So church is over and Dad says he's going to walk over to Riverside Drive, just for the exercise, and do me and Earl want to walk with him? I say yes, still being in my mellow mood, and Earl says no. So me and Dad start our little walk, and Earl goes into a candy store. I figured he's going to go in there to get some soda or something and do whatever he does when he's not around me.

Dad and I walk through the park, talking about nothing much, and I'm still mellow, and I'm digging the walk and everything. Then we go home, and he's talking about how it was when he was young, and I'm kidding him about how every generation always say they

48

had it so hard when they talk with their kids. Okay, everything's going along fine. Then I get home.

Mom's sitting in the kitchen drinking tea, and she's got this little smile on her face. Earl's cleaning the stove. Right away I'm shocked because Earl never lifts a finger to do anything.

"Earl said he felt bad about the way the boys left their room so he came home and cleaned it up," Mom says. "Made me sit down while he cleaned the kitchen, too."

I couldn't believe my ears. I went into our room and it was clean. The whole thing was spotless. I go back into the kitchen and Earl's asking Dad if he would like some tea. Dad sits there and says yes. I wanted to puke!

I went to church. I was mellowed out. I went for a cool walk. I was the one that wanted to clean the room in the morning in the first place. And I end up being the one that his bleeping lordship had to clean up behind!

This morning the minister was preaching about how we should seek understanding from God. Okay, that's cool. But until the understanding comes, I'll settle for revenge.

JULY 7th   Dear Twimsy:

When we got to Micheaux House today, we came right in the middle of a big argument between London and Mr. Santini. Santini was saying that London was the stupidest guy he had ever met in his life, and London was saying that Mr. Santini was the dumbest guy he had ever met. This was going back and forth pretty good, but you could see that Santini was getting the best of it because London was getting really mad.

"We are only using two bathrooms," Mr. Santini was saying. "That's so high a number for you to count? Two? One, two?"

Meanwhile Esther was crying, and the other women were trying to console her. We couldn't figure out what London had done, but right away Patty started signifying about how she always knew that London wasn't too bright in the first place.

"You ain't nothing but a misplaced jailbird," London said, pointing a big fat finger at Patty. "So just keep your fresh mouth out of this."

"You're fired!" Santini said, standing right in front of London. He was about half as big as London, and it looked as if London could have just reached over and swallowed him whole if he wanted to.

"How you going to fire me?" London asked. With his hands on his hips he looked like the Goodyear blimp with elbows. "You can't even fire yourself."

"No," Santini said, "but I can count to two."

"It don't matter how high you can count if you ain't got no toilet paper!" London said.

That's when we found out what it was all about, Twimsy. Esther Cruz had gone into the bathroom and used the toilet, and then she found out there wasn't any toilet paper. So she didn't know what to do, and she

50

stayed in the toilet until she heard some of the other women come by and then she called out to them. They went to get some paper from the other toilet, but London was in there and wouldn't give them any. So then they brought Esther some Kleenex or something, and she started crying because she was embarrassed.

The point, Twimsy, is that the city wants to close Micheaux House and most of the people have already moved out. Santini said that closing the place was like serving chicken instead of steak because it's cheaper—it makes a lot of sense to everybody except the chickens. The chickens in this case, Santini, Esther Cruz, and the others who haven't moved, don't really care about how expensive it is, they just want to stay in the old place. So what they're going to do is try to figure out a way of running the place by themselves. They say what they really want is a place they can think of as a permanent home, rather than just a place to stay. I think they're just set in their ways.

JULY 8th   Bad night. First Earl started hollering in his sleep and then, after he had scared me half to death with his hollering and my father had to come in and wake him up and everything and I had drifted back to sleep, he wakes me up and says he's got a problem.

"What's your problem?"

"The bed got wet."

At first I didn't know what he meant, but then I did. What he meant was that he had wet the bed again. When he had first come, he did that a couple of times, but he hadn't done it lately.

He looked real disgusted with himself, and I felt sorry for him—no, not really, I didn't feel sorry for him but a little with him, like it was our problem, not just his. I told him I'd get some clean stuff from the linen closet and for him to put the other stuff in the pillowcase and put it under the bed. We could take it to the center the next day and stick it in the washer and no one would know.

Sometimes I felt okay about Earl—at other times I wanted to break his neck. It's so different from what I thought it would be before he came. I imagined this cool little brother type hanging around and asking me questions about how to catch a baseball, that kind of thing. Also, I figured that he'd do just about anything I asked him to. What I got instead was a guy who was all set in the way he was and I was supposed to adjust to him as much as he was supposed to adjust to me. Earl's different from what I thought he would be, but I guess anybody would be. Maybe that's why people mostly adopt babies. You get yourself a baby and you know it's not going to give you a hard time.

JULY 9th   I don't know when the old people sleep. Whenever we get there, they're awake. Sometimes they take naps during the day, I know, but they're really short naps. By the time we get there at eight-thirty they're into their day already while we're still trying to wake up. We got there today and they're talking about jobs. They figure that if they got jobs they could bring in enough money to get by and then Micheaux House could stay open.

"Say, no offense," Patty said—she had on her silly little smile, "but how come you didn't think of that before?"

It was a good question, Twimsy, and caught us all by surprise.

"Because of you, mostly," Mr. Lasher said.

"What you mean by *that*?" Patty's voice rose sharply.

"Let me ask you something, miss." Jack Lasher was taking a Pepsi from the soda machine. He poured half of it into a plastic cup and took it over to where Patty stood leaning against the magazine rack. He gave it to her, and she smiled.

"What kind of work do you think I could do?"

"I don't know." Patty shrugged.

"Well . . . guess."

"Maybe a messenger or even a night watchman . . . something like that—I really don't know."

"How about Santini, what do you think he could do?"

"I don't know—why are you asking me?" Patty put the Pepsi down and caught an attitude. "I told you I don't know anything about jobs."

"How about you, my friend?" Mr. Lasher nodded toward Hi-Note.

"I don't think you could be a messenger because messengers really have to get around kind of fast, but you could be a night watchman or a doorman."

"You know what else you could be," I said. "One of those people who sells tickets at a movie or even one of the people who takes the tickets when you get in. That's pretty easy work."

"Anybody else have any other ideas?"

"A guy that shows you where to sit at basketball games," I said.

A school crossing guard was the last idea. Mr. Lasher asked us to keep thinking about it, but we really couldn't come up with any other ideas.

"I guess there aren't many jobs you can do," Hi-Note said.

"That's not true," Mr. Lasher said. "There's a lot of jobs we can do. Everybody here has worked all their lives. We all have skills, and we all have expertise of some kind. But when young people see us they don't see our skills—they see our age. What can an old man or an old woman do? I've done everything there is to be done in the construction field. There's no way I'm going to carry a hundred pounds of bricks up a ladder any more, but no one does this kind of bull work any more, anyway, even in construction. I could be useful in construction, but I had to retire when I was sixty-five because the union I worked in said I had to."

"How long were you in the union?" I asked.

"About forty years."

"They did you like that after you worked for them for forty years?" Patty asked.

"I thought they were doing me a favor," Mr. Lasher said. "I fought, I went out on a strike, I attacked a bunch of union busters with a sledgehammer once just to get that retirement clause into the contract.

"I had visions of myself being down in Florida and living next to the ocean. The money we fought for would have been great if we could have retired then."

"And who knew what old was going to be?" Eileen said, looking up from her racing form. "When I was a girl, forty was old if you weren't wealthy. When you reached forty or soon thereabouts, all thoughts of frivolity were put aside. Play was for children. So was love and sex. After forty it was all grit and duty. Now forty begins the second childhood for most people. You have enough money for vacations and sports equipment and what-have-you. The idea of a forty-year-old person buying a tennis racket for themselves in the thirties was considered an absurdity."

"So what you saying is that you can't get a job because no one is going to give you a job because you're old?" Patty asked.

"And because they think, like you young people, that all we can do is to sit quietly and perhaps move one arm to give a ticket or shuffle to a seat in a theater."

"I didn't mean anything personal," Patty said.

"You know, my man Earl was saying how we should get some jobs and help out." Hi-Note got into it.

"I ain't your man!" Earl said.

"Yeah, right, anyway, we can't get no jobs either." Hi-Note went on. "That's one of the reasons I didn't mind having to work here over the summer. At least it's something to do."

"I'm hip," I said. "We're all the same. Old people can't get jobs—"

"Seniors!" Mabel Jackson hadn't been talking at all, but when she opened her mouth she did it sharply. "Don't call us old people again."

"I don't see what difference it makes if we don't have any bad feelings about—you know—people who have . . . more years than us."

"If I call you 'colored' instead of 'black' does that make a difference to you?" Mr. Lasher asked.

"Yeah, but that's race," I said.

"No, it's not because it's race," Jack Lasher said. "It's because it's important to you. You claim the right to define yourself in your own terms. Well, we claim the same right. We want you to call us seniors."

"In fact, we insist on it!"

"Yeah, well, that's cool," I said.

"Now, what were you saying about us being all alike?" Mabel Jackson asked.

"Nothing," I said.

"He's offended." Eileen didn't look up from her crossword puzzle. She was always either working out her horses for the day or doing the crossword, and half the time she spoke she would be looking down at the paper. "People are always offended when you're insistent about being called something other than what they want to call you. I know I was certainly offended when I couldn't use the word 'colored' any more. It was such a *pleasant* word."

"Hey, cool out," Patty said. "Being old and being black are two different things."

"How would you know?" Mabel Jackson asked. "How long you been old?"

Well, Twimsy, that cooled things out for the rest of the day between the old—the seniors—and us. We didn't like them running down the race stuff, especially when we were just trying to help them. We all walked to the subway together at quitting time, and most of us, except for Earl, were a little ticked off. Everybody was mad except, like I said, Earl. He started running down some long story about how we didn't know what it was like being like them and everything.

"Well, how you know?" Hi-Note said.

"I just know," Earl said.

"Well, *how* you know, turkey?" Hi-Note stopped right in front of Earl. "How long you been old?"

"Since I been running around with your mama!" Earl said in a mean voice.

Now I knew that Hi-Note and Earl had been edging toward a showdown for a while, but I didn't think Hi-Note would jump up into Earl's face like that. I kind of stepped between them, and so did Patty, and the whole thing might have mellowed out with some hard looks if Patty hadn't stuck her two cents in.

"I'm sorry," she said, "but did you say you was going with his *mama*?"

Earl didn't say anything.

"Why don't you let it ride?" I said to Patty. "Don't be signifying."

"I just wanted to know if Earl was going with Hi-Note's mama," Patty said. "I ain't signifying, I'm just curious."

"Yeah, why don't you shut up?" Hi-Note said.

"Don't jump bad with me," Patty said with one hand on her hip. "*I* ain't going with your mama."

"You got to take it back," Hi-Note said to Earl.

"No, you got to make me take it back," Earl said.

Then they started fighting. Twimsy, they just started to fight because in two seconds the only one that was doing any fighting was Earl. Hi-Note swung first and hit Earl in the face. Then Hi-Note missed a punch and Earl was on him like white on rice. Earl hit Hi-Note in the nose and the blood spurted out, and then he hit him two more times before High-Note could grab his nose from the last hit. Earl was hitting three ways: fast, hard, and continuously. It didn't last more than a few seconds, I guess, but it was so bad that it seemed like longer. I learned something right then, Twimsy—that there's a big difference between what my father calls street kids and just regular guys. Hi-Note could just about beat anyone on our block, but he wasn't in the same league as Earl.

I didn't talk much to Earl after the fight until we got home. I told him that maybe he should try to make up with Hi-Note when we got to Micheaux House again. He said it was up to Hi-Note, because he was the one who started it.

"I know," I said. "The guy's been my best friend for years now, though. I just feel bad about the fight."

"You didn't do a whole lot to stop it," he said.

Twimsy, that was right, but when I started to say it really wasn't my responsibility, something like that, I could see it was the same as Earl saying that Hi-Note started the fight. I knew that when the fight was starting, but I didn't want to go against Earl or Hi-Note.

Earl had a bad night, tossing and turning until almost

daybreak. I didn't get much sleep either. How come I feel like the bad guy?

"How come you get so uptight about the old fo—the seniors?" I asked him in the morning as we dressed. "Like everybody wants to do something but you—you know."

He didn't answer me, and I wasn't sure if he had heard me or not, but I didn't push it.

JULY 10th   Dear Twimsy:

Hi-Note wants a return match with Earl, which I think is a definite mistake. What happened, I think, was that everyone was sitting around Micheaux House trying not to check out Hi-Note's black eye, and he figured he had to do something about it. So what he does is he tells Earl that he wants a rematch. But, hey, Twimsy, dig this. Earl comes over to me and tells me that he doesn't want a rematch. I'm shocked, but I try to cool things down.

"Let's just call it a day," I said. "We don't have to fight if we don't want to. Let's just forget about the fighting."

"I ain't forgetting about nothing," Hi-Note said.

"C'mon, Hi-Note," Patty said, "don't be like that."

"C'mon what?" Hi-Note winced a little when he turned toward Patty. The white part of the eye that was blackened was all bloodshot and looked more or less

59

awful. "You were the one that wanted to see a fight so bad yesterday."

Well, this went back and forth for a while, and you could see that Hi-Note was determined to fight. Now the way I figured, the only thing that was going to happen was that Hi-Note was going to get beat up again, because there was no way possible that he was going to beat Earl. Patty was trying her best to break it up, too, because she felt a little responsible for egging the fight on the day before, and she was.

The seniors were listening to part of the conversation, and when they figured out a fight was going on they had some suggestions, but they weren't much better than ours. Mabel Jackson and Esther Cruz just said that they shouldn't fight, that they should shake hands and make up, but I knew that wasn't going down. Jack Lasher said that they should put on boxing gloves, and that sounded like a bet until we figured out that no one had boxing gloves. London said what everyone else was thinking—that he couldn't see why Hi-Note wanted to get beat up again.

Now, while all this is going on, it's Earl who's keeping quiet, like he's the one that's afraid of getting beat up. To tell you the truth, Twimsy, I didn't want to see Hi-Note beat up again, because he was my friend and still is, but he was the one that was pushing it.

Hi-Note said that they would fight at noon, and everyone was sitting around watching the clock. I figured out that Earl, if he didn't want to fight, probably wouldn't hurt Hi-Note too much. At least I hoped he wouldn't. The way it turned out, though, I never found out.

Santini comes in about eleven-thirty, and he's got this paper that looks like some kind of official document, and he asks me if I could give him a hand with filling it out. Hey, that was cool because that was the first time any of the seniors had ever come out and asked for help like that. He said to come to his room and he had the other forms, and I went with him.

His room was smaller than I thought it would be, and as neat as a pin. Nothing was even dusty!

"What kind of form is it?" I asked.

"What form?" Santini asked.

"The form you want me to help you fill out," I said.

"Oh, that form." Santini took the forms and put them into a desk drawer. "I don't have any forms for you to fill out," he said. "I'm more interested in that fight. How did it get started?"

"Well, you know, Earl got all upset yesterday about what was going on here, you know, with the seniors."

"Yeah, I saw that."

"Anyway, he was mouthing off, and Hi-Note and he got into a little argument. Then I guess Patty egged them on a little."

"Patty? You tried to stop it yesterday?"

"Not exactly, but it was Patty who was doing the most talking."

"You know why he got so upset?" Santini asked.

" 'Cause that's the way he is," I said. "He's a little strange."

"Strange? Does he want to fight again?"

"No," I answered. "I guess he knows he can beat Hi-Note, so he doesn't want to bother."

"Could be," Santini said. "Then, on the other hand,

he might need a little nudge. Maybe if you went over to him and talked to him he wouldn't fight."

"No, man, you don't see," I said. "It's Hi-Note who wants to fight, not Earl."

"How could Hi-Note want to fight?" Santini had these little glass ships on his bureau, and he pushed them around with his finger as we talked. "He fought once and he got beat up—you think he doesn't know he's going to get beat up again if he fights again? Of course he knows. But his pride pushes him into the fight anyway. Only Earl can stop the fight. You go tell Earl to go to Hi-Note and tell him that he won't fight, and then Hi-Note can back down gracefully. Go ahead, you try that."

Okay, Twimsy, so I go and look around and sure enough there's Earl sitting and reading a magazine. I go over and sit next to him. Now, there had to be something spooky about the conversation between me and Earl. Maybe, if you put the words together just right they're magic or something. I don't know. I'm going to write the conversation down just as close to how it happened as possible.

Me: Hey, Earl, I got an idea.

Earl: What?

Me: Why don't you just go on over and tell Hi-Note that you won't fight him no matter what happens. That way he can back off. See, right now everybody knows you beat him, so his pride makes him want to fight again.

Earl: Yeah, I think I see what you mean.

Me: Yeah, he knows you beat him one time and now

he really doesn't want to fight you again, but he doesn't want to look like a chump that was beaten up.

Earl: I see what you mean, but if I go over there and say that, he's going to feel like everybody thinks I told him what I'd do to him or something and he's scared.

Me: So tell him out loud so everybody'll hear.

Earl: Right, and then he's going to say the same thing he's been saying all along. You people been saying things to him out loud and he keeps saying he wants to fight.

Me: Yeah, I guess so.

Earl: You right, it won't make no sense for him to fight me again, but he needs an out, you know, something that everybody can see, and it ain't got nothing to do with me.

Me: Right.

Earl: You think that's right?

Me: It sounds right to me.

Earl: Look, if he comes up to me to fight, why don't you step in and say you taking my place?

Me: Me fighting him doesn't make sense.

Earl: That's the point you was making, right? Then he can back off.

Me: I guess so.

Earl: You a deep dude.

The first time I fought Hi-Note, which was about three years ago, it only lasted about ten seconds and we mostly wrestled around. I'd say it came out about equal. This time he got the first punch in and landed it square on my nose. I was wondering how the heck I got into a fight with my best friend on a nice sunny day when I wasn't mad at anybody in the world. As it turned out, I wondered a little too long because he hit me again, and then we started wrestling around. But wrestling around on the ground was better than being hit. When you wrestled, you hardly even felt your elbows hurting until the next day. Your nose, that's a different story.

After the fight we went back to Micheaux House and cleaned up. London Brown heard about the fight and went after Hi-Note, asking how come he was always fighting. Hi-Note didn't say anything. London said that if he didn't stop fighting he was going to get sent to a detention center.

Twimsy, I was *glad* my nose bled, because everyone was oohing and aahing about that and nobody got much into why I had been fighting my friend in the first place. If somebody figures it out I sure hope they tell me.

JULY 12th   Twimsy:

I have to tell you some more about the seniors at Micheaux House. Mostly because of today, which involved Santini and Esther Cruz, but I have to start with the day before yesterday. Also, I got into it with my father, which I will tell you about later. But first let me tell you about some of the seniors.

Now, Twimsy, when I used to think about seniors, I thought about them as being a little slow and about how they walked. Most seniors don't bounce when they walk, like young people. That's true, but that's not always true, and it's not the most important thing about seniors, either. But that's a way of dealing with them in your mind, especially if you don't have to deal with them for real. You just get an image of a certain type, and then you make everybody the same. That's what I did with Earl before he got to the house. I got myself an image in my mind that I expected him to be like. When he wasn't, it was a shock—no, not a shock. Just hard to deal with. Because it ticked me off a little that he wasn't like the image.

I guess most groups are like that in my mind. All old people looked the same, all cowboys, all Martians if there are any, they're all the same. That's just the way those Iranians looked when I saw them on television during the hostage crisis—all the same. People can get kind of gray in your mind because you're not around them, in a way. When you are, it's different—you begin to see their personalities and things. Like Santini when he pulled out that sword and took on Hi-Note. When he did that you couldn't just think about him in the same way any more.

Okay, now, the day before yesterday we all get to Micheaux House and Eileen Lardner says that she has an announcement to make. Eileen is cool, but she turns everything into a number. Say, when she watches us play cards one day, and me and Patty beat Hi-Note and Earl. Earl says to Eileen that he and Hi-Note lost, and right away Eileen says that he and Hi-Note couldn't beat me and Patty more than fifteen percent of the time.

That got Hi-Note ticked off, and he insisted on playing a tournament. So we played a hundred games that week, and they only won thirteen. Hi-Note isn't that good really, and neither is Earl. I told Eileen that they only won thirteen percent so she could change her figure to that, and she said no, it was probably closer to ten percent but that me and Patty had been careless. That really ticked Hi-Note off even more, but there wasn't anything he could really do about it.

Anyway, that's the way Eileen is. She can add up numbers in her head faster than I can with a pencil and paper. Once I made a mistake on the adding machine, the right answer was ninety-nine and I got one seventeen, and she said I must have put a number in backwards, and she was right. It had something to do with the difference between the right answer and the wrong answer being divisible by nine. She had that kind of a mind. Other than that, she was pretty ordinary, tall for a woman and on the skinny side and with a regular face except that she had eyes that put you in mind of a cat's eyes.

When she said that she had an announcement to make, I thought it would have something to do with numbers, and I was right.

"Three hundred and fifty-seven dollars a month," she said, "is what will be required to keep this place going without city assistance."

After she went through all her explanations and things, it all came out to this: if the seniors wanted to go on living at Micheaux House, they would have to come up with another three hundred and fifty-seven dollars every month to pay for the gas and electric bill and things like that. And that was only going to be cool until it turned cold and the heating bills started coming in, she said.

"Well, it's a point of departure," Jack Lasher said.

"Which means that if we can't raise the money, we'd better be thinking of departing," Santini added. Everybody laughed at that, Twimsy, even though it really wasn't that funny.

There was a whole lot of talk about how we could raise the money, but nobody had a really good idea. But that number was good all by itself, because it was something concrete that we could talk about. Earl got back to his idea about us getting jobs and chipping in our money, but none of us knew where to get any jobs.

"You kids don't have to worry," Jack Lasher said. "I don't think the judge would have put you into a detention house for a day, let alone a month. I'm sure she's not going to put you into some place like that because this place closed."

"We were thinking about you," Patty said. "We want to help you."

"Us? You think we aren't capable of helping ourselves?" Lasher had on a gray sweater, and when he turned around from where he was sitting, he put his elbow right into some Coke that somebody had spilled on the Ping-Pong table. "We've been helping ourselves since before you or your father were born, kid." He wiped his sleeve.

"I didn't mean that you couldn't help—"

"Well, I've said what I mean," Jack Lasher said, cutting her off.

In a minute, maybe even less than that, Patty was

sulking. Nobody knew what to say for a while, or maybe, seeing the veins stick out on Jack Lasher's neck, they just didn't want to say anything. Finally Eileen went over and sat next to Patty and put her arm around her.

"Darling, it's not that we aren't appreciative of your concern," she said. "It's really quite lovely of you to want to help and everything. But the truth of the matter is that we are actually quite capable and we can do the kinds of things required to help ourselves as long as people don't get in the way. And just like you want to gain your own independence, we want to maintain ours. You *do* understand that, don't you?"

That was another thing about Eileen—anything she wanted, she would point out that you wanted it, too.

Patty said that she did understand, but I didn't, not exactly, anyhow. London Brown said he would help, and made a point of saying he was going to help because as long as the place stayed open, he had a place to live. I didn't even know he was staying at Micheaux House.

It was Patty's birthday and we all chipped in and took her to the Rib-'n'-Chicken Joint on Lenox. When we had eaten some ribs and fries, Patty went on about how she was right, that we were just trying to help the seniors and they shouldn't catch an attitude.

"They don't have to be kissing our hands and things," Patty said, "but they don't have to be so hard, either."

"When you go back to school, where they gonna be?" Earl asked.

"Wherever they are, I guess," Patty said.

"Right, and if they take it light or take it hard, it's

gonna be the same thing," Earl said. "They got to rely on themselves to get over!"

The conversation dropped there. Nobody really wanted to get into another argument with Earl.

Then, out of a clear blue sky, Patty says, "Watch me get a free rib." She calls over to this guy we call Crock who runs the Rib-'n'-Chicken and says that she's probably the only one in the whole world who can eat ribs faster than he can. Now this was a joke, because nobody in this world or the next can eat a rib faster than Crock. Crock is a light-skinned, skinny guy with gray eyes and just about no shoulders at all. He's got skinny hands and squinty eyes, and little ears, too. In fact, everything about Crock is little except his mouth. He got a big mouth like a crocodile. He can scare you to death just by smiling at you.

So when Patty says this, Crock just holds up a rib, gives her this big smile, and then snaps at it.

Now, he doesn't exactly eat a rib like most people. Most people take a rib in their hand and pull the meat off with their teeth. Crock, he puts the whole rib in his mouth and just sucks the meat off before you can blink. *That* fast. Zip—in goes the rib. Zip—out comes the clean bone—then zip-zip his Adam's apple goes up and down. Just like that.

"Uh-uh," Patty says. "That's because you don't have any competition. Let's both eat a rib at the exact same time so you can have some pressure."

I couldn't see how anybody could put pressure on Crock in a rib-eating contest, but Crock said okay. Patty goes over to Crock and lays down two napkins and tells him to put a rib on each napkin and to make sure that they're exactly the same size, which he does.

Then Patty clears her throat once or twice, and I see Crock looking at her, and he's getting a little nervous. He clears his throat, and when Patty leans over the rib and yells out for somebody to say, "Go," Crock does the same.

Earl yelled out, "Go!" and they both went for their ribs, only Crock takes a quick peek at Patty and gets his a second late. But once he gets it, it's no contest. Wham, it's gone. Patty hasn't even got her rib to her lips yet, and Crock's old Adam's apple has done its dip. But Crock is still bending over the napkin, and when Patty, who's also still bending over the napkin, looks up with the rib still in her hand, she's staring right at him, and he's got this little piece of meat hanging out of his mouth, and she starts to crack up.

She laughs so hard she has to put the rib down and sit down herself. Crock, he's going on saying how he's still the fastest rib-eater in Harlem.

"Ain't a man, woman, or child can beat Crock," he said, finally standing up straight. "I can beat a dog eating a rib!"

When Patty had finished two glasses of water, for her hiccups, she started on the rib—the one she didn't pay for!

I told Earl I'd catch him later and walked for a while with Hi-Note and Patty. When we dropped Patty off, me and Hi-Note walked a while farther without saying anything.

"Look, man," I said, "I really want to stay friends

with you. We don't have to let one thing mess us up."

"You showed where your friendship was when the deal went down," Hi-Note said, stopping and turning toward me. "I didn't say nothing to you or do nothing to you, and you jumped in the fight against me, so don't come sounding no garbage to me because I don't want to hear it."

"I didn't think you'd fight me," I said. "If you didn't fight me the whole thing would have ended differently."

"Yeah," he said, "and I thought we were too tight for you to go out of your way to fight me, but you did. So as far as I'm concerned, you can walk on the other side of the street from now on."

He turned and walked away, leaving me standing in front of a little storefront church.

"How come ya'll didn't fight?" A little long-headed kid was standing on one foot leaning against the building.

"We already did," I said, turning to leave.

"You musta lost!" he shouted after me. "You the one trying to make up!"

Dig it, Twimsy, the young people at Micheaux House want to help the seniors, but we ain't doing it right or something, so the seniors keep getting mad at us. We get mad because the seniors get mad. I want to make up with Hi-Note, but he's mad at me because I fought him to stop him from fighting Earl, who's mad at everybody but who claims to know more about the seniors than anybody else.

It's enough to make me mad!

So I go home and my moms is making dinner. She's

making some Italian dish, which she calls by some fancy Italian name, but which I call her Tomato and White Cheese Disaster Dish. She mixes hamburger, tomatoes, some white cheese, some noodles, and other stuff in a pan and bakes it. My moms can't cook at all. If I marry some girl who cooks like my mom, I'll have to join the Navy or something. And the funny thing about it is that if you say you don't like it she doesn't believe you. She thinks you're in a rut or something.

"Let your tongue live a little," she says.

When I eat her Tomato and White Cheese Disaster Dish, my teeth want to bite my tongue just to get even. One time, just to vary the fallout ratio, she served it with green mashed potatoes instead of noodles. The colors alone were enough to make you throw up. If she served it in a restaurant, the ASPCA would ban doggie bags.

I asked where my father was, and she says he's in bed. I wonder what he's doing in bed so early, and so I go into his bedroom, and he's lying on his side trying to read a magazine. I figure he's sick, but I don't ask what's wrong. I just ask how he's doing, and he says not too good.

"That's too bad," I said.

"By the way," he said, closing the magazine, "I think your mother and I have come to a decision about Earl."

"Oh, yeah?"

"It's unfortunate," he says, "but I just don't think he's going to work out."

"What's that mean?"

"It means that, after his trial period, he'll . . . we'll

have to let him return," he said. "I think it'll be better for everybody."

"Who's *everybody?*" I asked.

"Your mother, me, you, even Earl," he said. "We've given it a lot of . . ."

I walked on out of the room without letting him finish, and he came to my room a moment later and asked me what was wrong.

"Nothing."

"Something must be wrong or you wouldn't have walked out like that," he said.

"Why don't you just leave me alone!" I said.

"You don't talk to me that way," he said. "I'm your father, and right or wrong, I try to do what's best for you. This isn't an easy decision for me, son. I didn't take it lightly, no matter how it sounds."

"Well, right now I don't care if you took it lightly or if you took it hard, it still comes down to the same thing, doesn't it?"

"I didn't think you were that fond of Earl."

"I'm not."

"Well?"

"Well, why isn't he working out?"

"A number of things," he said. "We found out that he had a fight with one of the staff people at Micheaux House—"

"Who told you that?"

"I wish you had, but the court called Micheaux House to see how all of you were doing, and they passed the report on to me. There seems to be some kind of friction between the two of you—"

"We can work it out."

"I'm not sure about that, son."

"Are you sure about *anything?*"

He just looked at me for a long time and then closed the door.

JULY 13th   2 a.m. Can't sleep after talking to my father last night. I'm about as twisted over this thing as I can be. Also, I thought I was writing down just about everything in this journal. Not true. When my father said that he thought that we shouldn't keep Earl, some other things came up, things I had been thinking about in a way, maybe in the background. I know it's not like if Earl doesn't stay with us he's going to die or anything like that, but when you have the say about somebody, the responsibility for how they're going to be, it's hard. What I want, I think, is to not be responsible so that even if something happens that I want to happen, I can say I didn't *make* it happen.

You know what I wish? I wish I could start the summer all over again and there was no Earl Goins. I'd be playing softball, maybe a little basketball, maybe even get a part-time job or something. That's the way to spend a summer, not worrying about some guy that's not even a blood brother.

JULY 14th   Dear Twimsy:

I figured Mabel Jackson cried once in a blue moon. Eileen never cried, but every time you turned around Esther Cruz was boo-hooing. But this time Mr. Cool, otherwise known as Santini, was also upset. Now you figure like this, Twimsy, it's going to be pretty hard to goof up when you're just sitting around watching two people be upset, right? And it's even harder when the two people are seniors and the problem is between them, right? Wrong! I blew it. Picture it like this. Esther is sitting in the chair by the window and she's crying. Not a real loud boo-hoo, just a little sniffling, but she's going at it pretty good. All the seniors are pretty uptight, but Santini is pacing up and down the floor like crazy. The kids are all gathered around, too. You really hate to see somebody cry, especially an older person.

Santini's pacing up and down, and every once in a while he goes over to Esther Cruz like he wants to say something, but he just pats her on the shoulder and tells her not to cry. Finally Patty can't stand it any longer and asks what's wrong. I like that about Patty.

"Nothing," Santini says.

"He wants me to live with him," Esther Cruz says.

"He wants to *marry* you?" Patty asks.

"No, he just wants to live with me," Esther says.

That's when I cracked up. Because what happened is that Santini's business is in the street. He wants to shack with Esther Cruz.

"And what's so funny about that?" Santini turned red in the face as he turned toward me.

"Hey, I didn't mean anything by it," I said. "I know you just want to live with her because of companionship, that kind of thing. But the way it sounded it was like you wanted to live with her to . . . you know . . . fool around."

"That's why I don't want to live with him!" Esther said.

Then Patty cracked up. That was cool because it got Santini off my back for the moment and he turned toward Patty. By this time he was really turning red.

"Whatever it is that's so funny escapes me," Eileen said.

"You people can't live together to be fooling around," Patty said. "That's ridiculous."

"Why—why—is that ridiculous?" Santini sputtered.

All the kids were smiling by then, even Earl. We didn't want to say anything, but we couldn't stop laughing every time we looked at each other.

"Do you think it's funny that we want to—how do you put it?—fool around?" Santini asked. "You think the urge stops when you're finished high school?"

"I just never heard of senior citizens doing anything like that," Patty said.

"I never heard of you before I saw you," Santini said. "Does that mean that you weren't there all the time?"

"I thought when you were old there were things you couldn't do," Hi-Note said.

"Darling." Eileen didn't look up from her paper. "When you are a child, you walk the way a child walks. When you are an adult, you walk the way an adult does. When you are older, you walk the way an older person walks. You don't get where you're going as quickly, but

76

you manage quite nicely if you're interested."

"Why don't you just get married?" Patty asked, changing the direction of the conversation.

"Because the social security benefits, food stamps, everything goes down if you're married," Esther said. "It's too hard. But I don't want to live like that. I don't think it's right for him to ask me to do that."

"I don't want to talk about it," Santini said.

He stormed out of the room.

"If you ask me I think you should live with him, married or not," Eileen said. "I mean, you've been in love with him for ever so long, haven't you?"

"But men change if they live with you and they're not married," Esther said. "I had a cousin once who lived with a man. He gave her a long story about how they were too much in love to need to make it legal. They lived together for nine years, and then, after three children, he left her for a younger woman. But he got his in the end."

"What happened?" Patty asked.

"His new girl friend left him in three months for her old boyfriend, and then he came crawling back to my cousin. She made him beg her to marry him on his hands and knees—well, maybe just his knees."

"Did she marry him?"

"What else with three children?"

Twimsy, the conversation broke down about there with Eileen, Esther, Patty, and Mabel talking about this woman they knew or that one. It went on for the rest of the morning, and I wasn't a whole lot interested in it.

Later me and Earl were shooting some pool when

London came in, and we asked him about whether or not the seniors really fooled around.

"What else they got to do with themselves?" London said.

"I thought old people didn't do things like that," I said.

"They do it," London said. "Only the physical bit is not as important to them as it is to really young people. The caring for each other is more important."

"I can get next to that," Earl said.

"How do you know, turkey?" London said. "You too ugly to know anything about love."

Hey, Twimsy, guess what happened? When London said that, Earl just smiled. That's the first time that I had ever seen anybody play with Earl and him just take it like that. He had a nice kind of smile, but I was surprised to see him take it so easy. Especially when London brought up the bit about Earl's being ugly. I mean, he's not ugly, exactly. You figure like this, when they dropped the ugly bomb, it didn't score a direct hit on my man, but the fallout definitely got him.

When it was time to go home, I asked Earl if he wanted to shoot some baskets in the park, and he said okay, so we went over to the park and played some two on two with some lames we found over there. We beat them three games in a row, and then we played them fifty-two for a quarter a game. They beat us three games in a row. That's probably because we were so tired from beating them the other games. They got our seventy-five cents, but they still couldn't play basketball.

The reason I didn't want to go right home was because of what had happened between me and my father. I was sorry about what I had said—no, I wasn't sorry, but I was sorry for the way I had said it. Right, that's it. Wait. I was sorry for what I had said because it was like I didn't love my pop, and I guess I do. I mean, I really never thought that much about loving him, or my mother, really. That's your fault, Twimsy.

Dig on this. Before I started writing things down in this book I could say things that sort of missed what I was talking about. As long as they came close, it was cool. Like I could say about Earl, "I dig the cat," and it would be all right because what I meant by saying that would be kind of vague but all right. But when you write stuff down, you have to write closer to what you mean or the whole idea of writing it down doesn't make any sense. At least, it doesn't make any sense for me. That's what I mean about loving my father. Before I started writing this all down, I would have said, "Sure, I love my father and mother." Now I ask myself what that means. What does it mean when I say I "love" my father? Dig where I'm coming from, Twimsy? Anyway, I'm not going to get into it too deep just in case I come up shaky. I *want* to love my father, and I think I do.

Anyway, we got home and I had already decided to apologize to my father and everything, but nobody said anything. We had dinner, watched the tube for a while, then I went to my room and read. I figured if my father wanted to talk to me, he could come in when I was in the room and then I could tell him I was sorry. Only he didn't come in. Earl came in after a while and started drawing. That's a thing that Earl's kind of good at, only he draws the same things over and over again—these outdoor winter scenes. I asked him once why he didn't draw something else, and he said, "Like what?" I said, "Like a horse or something."

"You want a picture of a horse?" he said.

"Yeah."

"Draw one!"

JULY 15th   We got up in the morning and I saw that my moms was sitting around in the kitchen in her housecoat. Me and Earl were eating scrapple and grits when my father asks Earl if he'd tell the people at the center I'd be about an hour or so late.

"Yeah," Earl says, giving me a look.

I figured two things were going to happen. One, we were going to have a big talk about what had gone down between me and my father, or, two, my father was going to beat up on me. I mean, he hadn't hit me for almost two years, and I had just sort of figured that the hitting part was all over. But I had never said anything to him like that before, either.

I was really nervous by the time Earl left. My father poured himself another cup of coffee, and me, him, and my moms just sat around the table for a while. I wondered if he was waiting for me to apologize, but I couldn't bring myself around to it just then. Mostly because he had this way of using anything you say against you. He would say, "Who should pick up your dirty clothes?" for example. Naturally you knew you were supposed to say *you* should pick them up yourself, but when you said it he'd come back like he was really surprised—that kind of sarcasm thing. Anyway, I just waited it out, and then he started.

"I thought we should discuss what we started to the other night," he said.

"I'm sorry about what I said," I said.

"The thing is," my mother said, "is that it's working out a lot differently than we thought it would. What we thought we had to offer Earl just doesn't seem to be enough to fill his needs. And, to be fair, what we thought we would get out of it isn't exactly working out either."

"What *we* were going to get out of it?" My father looked at my mother with a surprised look on his face. "I don't know what that means. We weren't 'getting' anything out of bringing the boy into the house."

"We were, in a way," Mom said. There was a softness about her when she spoke the way she was that made me want to touch her.

"We were expecting to get a lot of good feelings from the whole thing," she went on. "The kind that you get when you know you've done something good and it all works out for the best. We've been lucky, really, and we're doing well, so we wanted to share that with someone. But we wanted the person, Earl, to be happy and glad that we were sharing—"

"I don't think so, Jessie," my father said. "We wanted to share and we certainly wanted the person to be happy, but I'd stop at saying that we were 'getting' something from it. That sounds like we were asking Earl for something in return, which we weren't."

"Then how come," I asked, "if we're not asking him for anything in return and we're so hipped up on giving him something—how come he has to go back?"

"That's not the point!" my father began.

"Yes, it is the point, and there's nothing wrong with that, I think." Mom was in her pre-sniffle period. "We have a family he has to fit into. And it's sad if he can't, but he has to fit or it just won't work out."

"Jessie"—my father took Mom's hands in his—"you're making it sound like our fault, and it isn't."

"He's certainly better than when he first came here," I said.

"So whose fault is it?" Mom asked.

"I just don't know what's getting into everybody!" My father was really upset. He gets these little good-doing speeches he wants to make, but when he gets upset he starts sputtering and then he can't finish them.

"Steve, what do you want?" my mother asked.

"I don't know," I said.

"You don't know!" My father hit the edge of his coffee cup with his hand and then knocked it over altogether, trying to keep it from tipping over.

"Richard, let's stop this conversation here," my mother said. "You're getting too upset."

Bad move. Never tell my father he's too upset, because then he really gets upset trying to prove that he's not upset. The first thing I know, he's yelling at my mother, telling her how he's the calmest person in the house and she's got her Joan of Arc look on her face like she doesn't care how hot the fire is, she can take it.

"Can we talk about this again?" I asked. "We all care about the whole thing, and I think we should talk about it more."

"I'm not too upset to talk about it now!" my father said.

"I think I am," I said. "And I want to kind of sort it out some more in my mind. I don't know what I want, really. I'm sorry about what I said to you the other day. I really am."

"Look." He slumped a little in his chair and exhaled. "I'm sorry it's come to this. No one means anyone harm here. It's important to me that Earl and I get along, but it's far more important right now that you and I can see eye to eye. Maybe I am too upset to talk about it right now. Let's have a bite to eat and put off talking about it for a while."

"Does that mean we won't make a decision until we have a chance to talk about it?" Mom asked. On the money.

"Okay," Dad said, "but just you and me, honey. It's our decision to make. If Steve doesn't object to the adoption, and I take it that he doesn't, that's sufficient input from him."

"I don't see why it can't be a family decision," I said. "It affects my life, too."

"Yeah, we'll consider that," he said, "but it's our decision."

We left it there, Twimsy. It was a little weird, hearing my father talk about wanting Earl to like him. I thought it should have been the other way around. I ran it down to Mom a little later.

"Everybody talks about kids trying to please their parents," she said. "But it's tougher the other way around, because you're the ones that leave us eventually. Think about it."

I put it on my checklist to think about in about twenty years. Right now I don't need any new problems.

Also, I asked Mom if she thought that Dad was right, that it wasn't my decision. She said that unless I didn't want them to adopt Earl, Dad was right. I don't agree.

JULY 16th   We got up late and Mom had already left so I told Earl to put on some toast. I find the eggs, and I'm just about ready to start making some scrambled eggs when I hear this funny sound coming from Earl. It's like there's something wrong with him, but he doesn't mind. He's kind of groaning but in a cool way.

"What's the matter, man?" I asked.

"What you mean, what's the matter?"

"How come you making that funny noise?"

"I'm singing. You ain't never heard that song?"

I asked him to sing a little more of it, and I recognized it as Smokey Robinson's big hit. I recognized it by the words, because Earl is not on speaking terms, let alone singing terms, with the melody. I figure the dude just can't sing. I'm not one to rub in someone's fault, but I thought I would drop a gentle hint.

"Earl, you know them dolls that say 'Ma-ma' when you press their stomachs?"

"Yeah?"

"Well, the last time I heard anything that sounds as bad as you do when you sing is when I heard four of them dolls that got caught in a garbage compactor."

That didn't go over very well, and we started talking about who could do what best. These are the things that I could do best:

1. Sing
2. Play baseball
3. Write
4. Fix things.

These are the things that Earl could do best:

1. Draw
2. Fight
3. Gymnastics.

The two things that we didn't agree on were pool and basketball. So we changed and went to the park and played two games of one on one. He won both games. Now, I didn't put in anything about reading or math because I didn't want him to feel bad. I only put writing in because he put in drawing. I figured if I beat him in pool I would leave it at that, and I said that we could play pool in Micheaux House.

We played one game of eight ball, and he was winning, but he scratched on the eight ball and I won.

Then I quit. He went on about how he had only lost on a technicality and stuff like that, which was right, but I didn't care.

Anyway, we were still fooling around the pool table when Mr. Lasher came in and we asked him if he wanted to play some pool. He said okay and played with us, and he could beat both of us. Earl isn't talking much and Mr. Lasher is going on about how when he was young if you played pool people would think you were a hoodlum, and no one had a pool table. Then Earl asks me if he can ask me a personal question. I said, "Go ahead."

"You ever kill anybody?"

"What?"

"You ever kill anybody?"

"No," I said. "You ever kill anybody?"

"No," he said, looking at the pool table. "How about you, Mr. Lasher? You ever kill anybody?"

"Yes," Mr. Lasher says in this calm voice. "I've killed people."

Twimsy, you could have knocked me over with a dangling participle, you wouldn't even need a feather.

"I figured you did," Earl says.

Then Mr. Lasher put his stick down and just walked away. I asked Earl what that was all supposed to be about, and he came up with one of his wise-guy answers. I kept on after Earl, but he was just acting cool and shooting pool. Then Mr. Lasher comes back, and he's got this photo album. Okay, here's what he runs down, the best I can remember it.

"We were in Camp Polk, and from there we went to

San Francisco and from San Francisco to Mindanao in the Philippines. There had been a landing there about a month before I got there. We moved north and we met the enemy.

"This is my unit." He showed us a group of about twenty guys posing for a picture. The picture was yellowed. There were other pictures on the page, too, mostly of one or two guys. Some were holding rifles, and one had a bottle of liquor and was holding it up.

He kept on turning the pages, and there were more pictures, some of machine guns, some of other kinds of guns. Most of the guys looked pretty happy.

"You didn't have no black guys in your outfit?" Earl asked.

"The army wasn't mixed then," he said. "Black guys mostly did the dirty work. They didn't do much of the fighting."

"How did you kill a guy?" I asked.

"Most of the time you just shoot at sounds in the army," Mr. Lasher said. "Especially over there. You'd hear some noises, and you shot into the trees and hoped you hit something before whatever you heard got you. Then one day we were sitting around and one of the guys got hit. They'd have snipers in a tree. When they left an area, they would leave snipers in the trees, and they would stay there for a day or so and then start picking guys off until they got themselves killed. One of our guys got hit and we were all under cover. We shot at the trees and nothing happened. I was lying on the ground behind a log. The log moved a little, and I thought there was another GI on the other side. Somebody finally got the sniper, and we got up, and I didn't see anybody on the other side of the log. I told a couple of the guys to back off for a minute, and I put a few shots into the log. When I did that, we heard a yell, and I shot into the log some more. It was one of their soldiers, a young Japanese guy, younger than me. I was thirty-two at the time, so he must have been about twenty."

"You get a medal or anything?"

"No, all I got was a good look at a guy I had killed. There was a life and it was gone, and I was the one that did it."

"It wasn't your fault," I said.

"Yeah, that's what I figured out the problem was," Mr. Lasher said. He closed the book and there were tears in his eyes. "That's what the problem was. There should have been anger. I should have been mad at a man I killed."

"How about Pearl Harbor?" I asked. "You know they started it."

"Yeah, could be," Mr. Lasher said. "But about ten, twelve years ago I went downtown to a place on Hester Street. They had a handicraft show there, and I'm kind of interested in that kind of thing. I met this Japanese guy, and we got to talking, and I invited him to stop with me for tea. He had been captured on Bataan and brought to this country as a POW. Then after the war he became a citizen. We sat down and we had tea and we talked, and he wasn't mad at me and I wasn't mad at him. But most of the guys in that album are dead just the same.

a certain amount of capital to start up. Eileen's coming into the inheritance is an absolute godsend."

"You still haven't said what kind of business it's going to be," I said.

"We've got two ideas," Santini said. "We can start a housecleaning business, or maybe office cleaning. Office cleaning is better. If we can get to clean maybe three or four offices on a regular basis, I think we can manage to get by. We could clean the offices at night, and we could take our time as long as we didn't bite off more than we can chew. And if we traveled around in threes all the time it would be relatively safe.

"The other business was the sandwiches and coffee business. You know that supermarket on Eighth Avenue?"

"Yeah."

"Well, they have a deli section there that's doing very badly. In fact the owner says that he's thinking of taking it out altogether. If we sold coffee and sandwiches from that deli, it would do two things. It would give us a place to work in, it would bring more traffic into the store, and it might even revive some of his deli business. If it caught on, it could be a healthy business."

"Is everybody going to chip in or just Eileen?" Patty asked.

I hadn't thought of that. When Patty first said it, I thought maybe she shouldn't have, in case they hadn't thought of that yet. But then Eileen cleared the whole thing up.

"The three thousand dollars, if I leave this place, wouldn't last me more than six months," Eileen said.

"You know what he told me?" Mr. Lasher stopped to blow his nose. "He said that when he was captured he hadn't killed anyone yet that he knew of. He hadn't seen a man fall, hadn't looked into a dead face. He said he thought that the GIs that caught him might have killed him, but he had that consolation. That one thing, that he hadn't looked into a face that he had killed."

"I'm sorry, man," Earl said. "I saw the pictures of you in your uniform and things . . . you know."

Mr. Lasher let us look through the book some more. He said we could so we did, but there was a funny feeling that both me and Earl got. Most of the guys in the pictures were smiling and looking right at the camera as if they were trapped in the pictures, or maybe in the time. I looked up once at Mr. Lasher, and he was looking at me, not the pictures.

Later when we left, I asked Earl what he thought about it, and he said that he had thought that if Mr. Lasher had killed somebody in the war he would be proud of it.

Twimsy, I asked Earl how he could think a stupid thing like that, and Earl just shrugged and got quiet. It wasn't the right thing to say, because when I thought about it I knew I would have thought the same as Earl.

We get home, and Mom is there, and she says there's just one piece of chocolate cake left, and who wants it? I said I didn't want it, and so Earl ate it. I'm not going to compete for a piece of chocolate cake in my own house from my own mother, that's for sure!

JULY 17th   Dear Twimsy:

Dig this. Patty's cousin Eddie had a tryout with the Yankees! They took him and about a dozen other guys to Yankee Stadium on an off day and they hit against Rudy May and then they hit against Gossage. Eddie said he hit three ground balls to the infield and got one line drive to center. Then they got to do some fielding. Eddie's an infielder and he said he didn't make any errors and his throws to first were good, too. If he makes the club he'll go to one of their farm teams. *All right!!!*

I think Micheaux House is getting me down. I miss playing ball something awful. I asked Earl wasn't it boring to be in Micheaux House, and he said it was better than being in the detention center. Well, anybody could have said that. It was probably better than hanging upside down by your big toe, too. But it was still boring.

It rained today like maybe it was going to be the end of the world. If it rained for forty days and forty nights like this it would definitely be the end of the world. Anybody who didn't drown would shrink to death. Patty said she saw a fish in the corner store buying an umbrella.

But the mood in Micheaux House was definitely up. Mostly the seniors are kind of quiet, but they were really going at it today. Santini had his sword out and was showing Esther how he had fought some guy, maybe thirty years ago, and everybody was generally smiling and talking to each other in a cheerful way. What happened was this. Remember that number I said Eileen had come up with? Well, the seniors had been trying to think of ways that they could come up with

the money. They figured that if they had s[...] to start with it would be easier to get some [...] Eileen said that she had a small inheritanc[...] had never bothered about, and she called t[...] find out how much it was. It turned out to [...] over three thousand dollars.

"We thought if we could get some money [...] we could somehow invest it or have it work for [...] we all have skills, things that we've picked up [...] lifetimes which we can do as well or better t[...] body else. The problem is how to make these sk[...] for us."

"You talking about getting jobs again, right[...] said.

"Not exactly," Jack said. "We know that most [...] won't hire us because they think we're too old."

"Or because their insurance companies think [...] too old, or because their pension fund insists th[...] the employees be in the fund until they're sixty-fiv[...] because of *this* or because of *that!*" Eileen said. "[...] it all boils down to is that no one is going to hire u[...] anything that we can make a living at."

"So we decided to hire ourselves," Jack Lasher c[...] tinued. "We figured that the people who know our val[...] most was us. So if we started our own little busine[...] and operated it, we wouldn't have to worry about an[...] body talking about our ages."

"You mean you're getting into the inheritance bus[...] ness?" Patty asked.

"No, but what was stopping us before was the idea [...] that any business, no matter how small it is, has to have

"Then what would I do? You see there's a point at which one must realize that our greatest resource, perhaps our only true resource, is each other. Don't you think so?"

"If you say so," Patty said.

"If you're not afraid of risking a headache," Eileen said, "try to think about it."

"I just decided," Patty said, and you could see that she was mad. "I'm not going to get old. I just scratched that off my list of things to do! No way I'm getting old!"

"Join the club," Mabel said. "Join the club."

Earl was the first to volunteer to help the seniors in whatever they decided to do. The next guy was Hi-Note. Then everybody else said they would help. You could see that the seniors were glad about us volunteering. It was almost as if they wanted us to approve of what they were doing. Santini said the seniors would have a meeting later that day to decide just what they wanted to do and we were invited to come. I was all for that and even asked when the meeting was going to be held, but then Patty says that she won't come, that whatever the seniors decided would be cool with her, and soon we were all saying that.

Hey, Twimsy, some funny things were going down at Micheaux House when all this was going on. Check it out. First, Earl was the first guy to volunteer, which I expected, but then Hi-Note jumped right in, and then I noticed that Hi-Note was sitting next to Earl. Later, when I was showing Patty what Jack Lasher had showed me in checkers, I dug Earl and Hi-Note rapping together.

Now, Hi-Note had been my Main Man. My Ace from

Inner Space. My Grit and Spit Brother, My Get Down Partner, A True Believer, My Brother Bad When the Times Were Sad, and the Jamming Trans to My Slamming Fusion. So, in order to cool things out with him and Earl, I jumped on his case and blew my thing with him while he and Earl are getting a thing going. Santini said that most of the stuff you did right went by the boards and you didn't get any credit for it whatever, and I can dig that. He didn't say anything about the Good Samaritan getting his feelings hurt.

Okay, Twimsy, a second thing. You know, I've been trying to figure out what was best for the seniors, and trying to figure out what was right here and what was right there, and whatnot. So how come when I wanted to go to the meeting and help plan the action I was the only one not to see that they wanted to pull the show off themselves? Tomorrow I'm not going to say a thing to anybody. If anybody wants me to do something, they're going to have to come up to me and ask me please to do it.

Another thing, I'm not going to go up to Hi-Note and say anything to him about him talking to Earl, either. I'm not even going to mention it to Earl.

JULY 18th   Dear Twimsy:

Earl said that Hi-Note just came up to him and started talking to him.

94

"You didn't say anything to him first?" I asked.

"No," he said.

JULY 18th (again)   Santini and London Brown took the television down from the shelf and they're fiddling around with it to get a better picture. Then London had to go somewhere and Santini was still messing with the picture. He got a pretty good picture and started to put the television back on the shelf. I went over to give him a hand and he asked me what I was doing. I said I was giving him a hand.

"Did I ask you for a hand?" he asked.

So I sat down and he put the television back by himself. The heck with him. The next time the television could fall on him and I wouldn't lift a finger.

A guy called Earl in the evening to come play some Ping-Pong. He asked me if I wanted to come, and I said no. The guy was someone he knew from the place he was staying. I asked him, while he put on his sneakers, what the place was like.

"Just a place," he said. "Got these big rooms with about six beds in each one."

"What do you do there?"

"Play Ping-Pong and checkers," he said. "That kind of thing."

"That's all you do?"

95

"Talk."

"About what?"

"Getting a place to stay, mostly."

Twimsy, you know what the place sounded like? Micheaux House.

JULY 19th   Dear Twimsy:

Jack Lasher got a call from his son who said he was on his way to visit him. Jack got real ticked because his son hadn't visited him in over two years.

"I get a card every Christmas and a follow-up call every Easter," Jack said out of the side of his mouth. "The kid's all heart."

When Jack had been talking about his son, he'd kept saying kid, but when the guy showed up with his wife, he was older than my father!

"Hi, how you been doing?" Jack Lasher's son was tall, and nothing seemed to fit on his face. He looked almost like Jack, and Jack was really kind of good-looking, almost like those guys you see in cigarette ads, only older. His son had just the same kind of a face, but everything was just a little off. Mostly it was the color, I think. Jack was about medium complexion for a white person, while the son was splotchy-looking. Some parts of his face were very white and the other parts were reddish-looking. Plus he was tall, a good six inches taller than his father. He looked potsy, though, as if he had never played any kind of sport.

"I don't have a lot of time," his son said, "but I didn't want to miss seeing you. Maybe we could go to your room."

"I don't want to go to the room," Jack said. "I spend too much time there already."

"Well, okay." Jack's son rubbed his nose with the palm of his hand. "How've you been doing? You look pretty good."

"I'm doing okay," Jack said. "How're you doing?"

"Okay, pretty busy at the office," Frankie said. "You know how that goes."

"Yeah, I know how it goes," Jack said, looking toward the window.

"Jo-Anne's been thinking about you a lot, haven't you, Jo-Anne?"

"I really have been." Jo-Anne was sitting on the couch. She was plump with a pretty face and wide eyes like a doll's. "This is a nice place. I didn't know they had kids here, though."

"They're just helping out over the summer," Jack said. "Nice bunch of kids."

"Hey, guess what," Frankie said. "We're thinking about getting a place on the shore—you know, a summer place."

"That'd be nice, get the kids out of the city. I'd like that."

"It's just a small place," Frankie said.

"I wasn't asking to come live with you, Frankie."

"I didn't say you were . . ." Frankie looked around the room. "I mean it's just a small place, that's all."

"Yeah, sure, I didn't expect you to buy a mansion," Jack said. "You know what you can put around it? Those

97

bonsai trees. You know they'd make it look nice and probably bigger, too."

"It's got a fence, one of those wire jobs," Jo-Anne said. "I'm not really good with plants and things."

"I've got a friend who's really good with—"

"Look," Frankie said, "I gotta run, big sales meeting tomorrow, but I got to tell you how really terrific you look."

"How are the kids?"

"Great, you wouldn't believe it. Jo-Anne'll send you pictures," Frankie said. "You got pictures you can send, right, honey?"

"I'll send the Little League pictures."

Jack walked them to the front door. I thought he would be a little down when he came back, but he was okay. He came over and said that his grandkids were really great.

"Have them come up here," Earl said. "We'll teach them how to use spray paint."

JULY 21st   Dear Twimsy:

The project that the seniors were working on turned out to be a lot of little projects instead of one big one. Part of this was because they included London in the deal. Now, London isn't a senior, but he was one of the few who kept on working right through even though it meant a cut in pay for him. London is struggling in night school, taking up Refrigeration Repair, and it's a little hard for him. Jack Lasher is giving him a hand. I also found out that the reason that London lives at Micheaux House is to save money so he can marry this girl from his hometown. He figured that he could save his money and work on getting a better job, and that way he wouldn't have any trouble making it with his wife.

When Jack Lasher started outlining the project, which they decided would be the sandwiches in the supermarket, London said that everybody couldn't work on that little job. He was right, too.

So me, Patty, and Mabel and Santini were going to work the fast-food thing. Santini had owned his own grocery store for thirty-two years and knew about buying meats and things like that. I thought if you were into something for that long it was just about forever, but even that came to an end, I guess. Santini and Mabel were going to make the sandwiches, and they bought a coffee maker, which was supposed to be me and Patty's job. I liked it.

Instead of office cleaning, Jack and London Brown went around to all the businesses in the neighborhood and got them to pitch in three dollars a week to have the sidewalk in front of their places cleaned. It came to nineteen stores that wanted their places cleaned and four that didn't. Jack said that when the others saw that the whole block was keeping their places clean, they would shape up. That came up to fifty-seven dollars a week, but it wasn't that much work. Earl, Jack Lasher, and London took care of that job, and also Jack got some of the stores to let us paint new signs and put them up for them. That was a one-shot deal, Jack said, but good advertising, and we made fifteen dollars on each sign.

Esther, Eileen, and Hi-Note did the bookkeeping and also were to do most of the cleaning up around Micheaux House.

The big money-maker figured to be the sandwiches, and they invested about a thousand dollars in that project. Some of the money went for the coffee maker, which cost nearly a hundred dollars, some went for meats and other supplies, and the rest went for future supplies. They had to give the guy who owns the supermarket twenty dollars a day. Santini said this was a pretty good deal because the guy had agreed to the arrangement for eighteen months.

"It's a lot cheaper than having to pay rent for a place and insurance and redecorating the place," he said.

They invested some money in brooms and paints for the signs and things, and then Eileen lent a thousand dollars to London Brown. London had an old Lincoln Continental that he said got about one block to the gallon and made a noise like there was a hatchet fight going on under the hood. With the money he got from Eileen, he bought five used waxing machines and some other supplies and started his own waxing business with some guys he knew.

Some of the seniors were a bit leery about giving London that much money, but Eileen made the decision more or less on her own, and it was her money. London was supposed to repay the money and ten percent of the profit he made. In turn, Eileen was going to keep his books. I didn't know if that was a good deal or not, but I figured if Eileen wanted to do it, it would be okay. Personally I don't think London is that bright, anyway.

JULY 28th   Dear Twimsy:

I haven't written for seven days, and I've got a lot to tell. Dig this. Today is Thursday. Last Friday my pops comes into the room when me and Earl are lying over the edge of the bed digging television upside down, see. No big deal, just wanted to see if we could see anything different. Patty said that she stood on her head once and watched *Family Feud*, and she thought she saw the announcer giving signals to one of the families.

Anyway, in comes Pops and asks if we would like to do something different for the weekend.

"Like what?" I asked.

"I thought it would be nice to take a camping trip," he said.

A camping trip? Twimsy, this dude don't even like grass. When we go to a restaurant, he won't even eat a salad unless it's shrimp cocktail or something like that, because he says it reminds him of grass. Okay, so now he says he wants to go on a camping trip, and you get the picture of him reading in some magazine where it's a good idea to take your kid on a camping trip.

When he asks, I'm supposed to say something good-

doing like, "Gee, Dad, that's a great idea!" So I said
something like that, and then he asked Earl and Earl
said okay. It's supposed to be just the three of us. I also
figured that it had something to do with our conversation about Earl before. I don't know what this is supposed to show, but I go along with it. So he has us get
up and go downtown with him to Herman's and we buy
about one hundred and twenty dollars' worth of gear.
Plus, I still had a lot of my stuff from when I was in the
Scouts. Okay, so we're supposed to get up early and go
to this place in Pennsylvania that he knows about.

JULY 28th (continued)   Early? The moon was still out,
and he's shaking us and talking about hop to it and stuff.
I looked at Earl when he went out of the room and Earl
looked at me and we both laughed. Okay, so a-hunting
we will go.

We hop into the car and drive for three hours, and
we come to this place, and there's this guy he knows.
Get this, when we get to this place it's about seven-
thirty. Seven-thirty! We leave the guy and the car behind, and off we go into the woods. We have a compass
and Dad is talking about how it's up to me and Earl to
figure out which way we're going so we don't get lost.
I figure like this, how lost can you get in Pennsylvania?
The worse thing that can happen is that you find the
road and have to stop at an emergency stop to ask the
police where you are.

102

Every once in a while we stop and my father points out something that we might have missed, like a huge dead tree lying right in front of us or something like that. We go on like this, walking through the woods until it's noon and I'm about as tired as I can get. I figured we'd do this for a while and then play a few games about how we're lost and get back to the car, or we might even stay overnight in the woods since Dad really seems kind of gung ho about the whole thing. I'm laid back, but Earl is getting a little uptight. And soon I realize that he really thinks we're going to get lost. My man keeps checking out the compass and looking around as if he's nervous. Then it comes to me, when Earl was first staying over to the house he couldn't sleep with all the lights off. If we stay overnight, the sucker might freak out.

Dad's walking about twenty yards or so in front of us, and I run up to him and call out something about what kinds of birds we're hearing.

"What kind of birds do you think they are?" he asks.

"Hey, look," I said, keeping my voice low. "I never told you this, but Earl sleeps with the light on. He really gets upset when it's really dark out. I just wanted to let you know in case you were thinking of spending the night out here."

We walked on for a while longer, maybe fifteen minutes, and then Pop stops and says let's break for lunch. So we break out the food that Mom made—sandwiches, fried chicken, and jars of potato salad. I didn't know how long the food was supposed to last, but knowing my mother, I knew she'd pack at least twice as much as we'd need.

After we finished lunch and made sure that we didn't leave any garbage around, Pop turns to us and asks which way were we headed mostly. I looked at Earl, and he looked at me.

"I don't know," I said. "Which way do you think?"

"We must have gone a little of every way," Earl said. "I ain't too tough on these compasses."

Hey, Twimsy, can you dig the idea of my father getting us lost? Well, that's what we were. Okay, so we start walking due east. We're walking and talking and just being cool, and we're not getting anywhere that looks like anything, see. Then we take another break and eat up the rest of the food.

"We gonna sleep out here?" Earl asks.

"Well. What would you like to do?" my father asks, being cool.

"It don't make me no difference," Earl says.

"Oh."

That from my father. Now he thinks maybe he was wrong, or I was wrong, about Earl being afraid of the dark. So he talks about when he was a kid and he was in the Scouts and whatnot, and meanwhile Earl is eating it up. Now my old man sees this, and he's going on because Earl is digging it, and it's like I'm not even there. We finish eating and we start putting up the tents. Now this is cool, and I kind of like it, but my father and Earl are really getting off on the whole thing. We pitch two tents, one for Earl and me and the other for my father. For the rest of the evening we just sit around and rap a little, with my father doing most of the rapping.

We made a fire, but it wasn't what you would really call a Boy Scout fire. We gathered some dry sticks and a few logs, but we had to light it with a cigarette lighter.

When it got dark, it really got dark. I have never seen it so dark that the darkness comes right down and gets on you, but that's how it got, Twimsy.

We had trouble keeping the fire going, and before you knew it, the blaze, which wasn't anything to brag about in the first place, had died down.

"Make sure you tie your tent flaps down good," my father said.

"How come?" I asked.

"In case any animals start nosing around in the dark," he said.

Thanks. I needed that.

Twimsy, I'm not afraid of New York City darkness. New York knows how to get dark. The sun goes down, and you can say, "Hey, it's dark," but New York doesn't get ridiculous about it. Out there in the woods it got ridiculous! You could bring your hand toward your face and not know how close it was until your nose got bumped. I figured Earl must have been glad to be sleeping with me instead of alone.

Also, in New York the noises are cool. Maybe you hear a truck going past. Once in a while somebody passes with a loud radio or they're laughing. Those are cool noises. Out in the woods you hear little chirping noises and things screeching. Then sometimes you hear a rustling noise that *could* be the wind. It could also be some long-haired, red-eyed thing with yellow teeth that ran around eating dudes that worked in Micheaux

House. I was sure Earl was going to get nervous and start a conversation or something.

"Hey, Earl, how come, when you were at that place, you guys talked about getting a place to stay so much?"

"I don't know," he said. "Just did."

"Yeah, but why do you think they did it so much?"

"I think I'm tired," he said, "and I want to go to sleep."

"Tired? How come you're scared to sleep with the lights out back home and you don't care out here?"

"I ain't scared of nothing," he said. "I just don't want my enemies sneaking up on me."

"They could get you out here," I said reassuringly.

"I'll take a chance. Go to sleep."

Then he went to sleep. I got another thing against Earl. He's unreliable.

My father was the first one up in the morning and he woke us up by banging on the top of the tent and yelling something that I guess he thought was funny about the Russians coming down the road. I don't know why he thought that was funny.

He took the tents down and rolled them up, and then we found out that we didn't have any water left. That is, we had a little water but not enough to make it through the day. My father took the compass and we started due east again. I asked him why we were going east and he said because since most of the industrial areas were in the East, the woods probably didn't continue as far in that direction. Good thinking.

Me and Earl talked some on the way, mostly about Micheaux House, and it seemed that he was really interested in it. Meanwhile, my father put on this real cool voice, the one he usually put on when he thought it was time to panic and didn't want anybody else to know.

"Lovely day, isn't it?" he said.

"It's going to be another lovely night in these woods, too," I said.

He smiled a little, which was cool, but I knew he was lost, and I told Earl.

"That ain't no big deal," Earl said. "We ain't lost."

"You know how to get out of the woods?" I asked.

"Nope."

"Then how come we ain't lost?"

"'Cause we ain't got no place to go," Earl said. "If we had someplace to go in a hurry, then we would be lost. We can hang around in the woods all day and it don't mean a thing."

We didn't reach the road until almost eleven-thirty. My father stopped a car and asked how far it was back to the camp. The guy in the car said it was about five miles but that he would give us a lift if we wanted it. My father asked us if we wanted to take a ride with the guy, but me and Earl both said we'd just as soon walk, so we started walking down the road in the direction the guy pointed.

Twimsy, I don't know how long five miles is, but if that was five miles, then I would hate to walk ten miles. We walked until my knees were beginning to hurt. When we finally got to the camp, the guy who knew my father said that we had had quite a trip for ourselves. I'm hip.

We also found the other water bottle in the back seat

of the car. On the way home we stopped at McDonald's, and my father asked us how we liked the trip.

I said it was okay, but Earl started talking about how he really dug it, and I could see that he meant it, too. My father was digging on Earl's liking the trip, and they were really rapping to each other.

I had a feeling, right then and there, that my father was going to adopt Earl. My mother had said that there was something we wanted to get from Earl, and I hadn't really known what she was getting to, but checking out my father there I could see he was getting something from Earl now. Maybe now that I was almost grown, he was trying to find a way to be like those fathers on television or something. He couldn't really be that way with me, I guess.

Twimsy, it wasn't that I didn't like the trip, it was just that I figured my father was trying to get some point over with it and I was trying to check it out. When we got home, Earl took a shower and I wanted to talk to my father, but he was talking to my mother. Then she asked Earl, when he came out of the shower, how he had liked the trip. She asked me, too, but it was like she thought she should ask, not that she wanted to.

Earl fell asleep later, and I got a chance to ask my father what the trip had been about, and he ran down some stuff about how he thought two growing boys would like to go on a camp-out. Then I asked him if it meant that now he was for adopting Earl again.

"Steve, I'll tell you two things. One, you're right in thinking that I feel more favorably about adopting Earl now. But what I wish is that I'd get some kind of a sign or something, a big flashing neon yes or no. I'm a father, and that's how I have to think. It's got to be an objective decision. Can you understand that?"

I told him that I did. What I didn't tell him was that I was beginning to get annoyed with him because he kept flip-flopping back and forth. It's aggravating to have people do that, especially your father.

JULY 29ᵗʰ   Twimsy:

The first day of the project Santini had chest pains and they had to call the doctor. He's got something called angina, and when he gets really excited he gets these terrible chest pains. They think that the pains aren't too serious (except for the fact that they hurt a lot), but they can never be sure he's not having a different type of attack. So everybody sat around and waited until the doctor came out from examining Santini and had given him something to ease the pain. Esther Cruz was really upset, and by the time lunchtime came around, they had to give her some medicine to calm her down.

"Maybe he shouldn't take part in the project," Patty said. "It's good to get the jobs and everything but, you know, if he's got a bad heart . . ."

"There's lots of reasons folks stop living before they die," Mabel Jackson said. "Him having a bad heart ain't no reason for him to sit down and make believe he's dead before his time. If we were going to do that, we wouldn't have to worry about nothing. That's what we're trying to get away from."

"From sitting around doing nothing?" I asked. "That doesn't sound so bad to me."

"That's because you can sit around and do nothing if you want to," Mabel went on, "or you get up and do something if you want to. People expect senior citizens to want to sit around and do nothing all the time. They think we done had our time to do, and this is our time to sit and wait for the undertaker. If you sitting and staying out of their way, they are glad, and if you're lying down in one of them prison beds they got for you, they are even gladder."

"I don't think anybody wants to see you lying in bed," Patty said. "I was just afraid that if Santini had a heart attack something might happen."

"Something? What kind of something? Only something that can happen with a heart attack that people be afraid of is that they going to die. People don't want us to move around too much because if we die it reminds them they got to die sometime, too. People get mad if you even talk about dying."

"I didn't say anything like that," Patty protested.

"Don't get touchy, girl," Mabel said. "I didn't say you did. You young enough so that you can figure you might not never die. You ain't scared of dying yet, leastways you shouldn't be. But you don't know what it is to have to deal with the folks we be dealing with. They don't want you to talk about being old because

110

they don't want to get old. What they want to do is to fit you into a nice little box like a television or something and then tune you in and out when they have a mind to."

"They may feel that way sometimes," I said. "But they probably have your best interests at heart. I mean, I don't dig a lot of talk about dying either, but I don't want to put you in a box."

"That's 'cause you some sweet children," Mabel said. "Another thing, you ain't making no living on old folks. You making a living on us and you see things different. Take this place—you know why they closing it down?"

"The guy said it was more efficient to run one large place rather than a lot of neighborhood places."

"The real reason they closing it down is because not enough people be lying in bed staring at the ceiling," Mabel said.

"They get more money from the government if you're sick in bed," Eileen said. "It's the only thing that keeps some of these places running."

"You know," Patty said, "I don't believe that. I mean, about them getting more money if you're sick and stuff."

"Girl, let me tell you something," Mabel said. "If you poor or old or if you black or if you a woman, you better be about knowing things that don't mean you no good. If they's more money in you being a dog than a human being, you can bet somebody going to try to put a collar on your neck. And you can take it from me that I didn't get to be no old dried-up woman like I am by being nobody's fool!"

"Is she hip?" Eileen asked.

"What's that mean?" Hi-Note asked, cocking his head to one side.

"Isn't that what you say when you agree with something?" Eileen asked. "That you're hip?"

"Yeah, yeah." Hi-Note grinned. "You're hip!"

JULY 30th   Twimsy.

I had a heart-to-heart with Moms in the supermarket. We were picking up some odds and ends, mostly about fifty kinds of soap stuff. She has one kind of soap powder for clothes, one kind for dishes, one for the bathroom, and two kinds of soap, one regular and one clear.

"Did your father have a chance to talk to you again?"

"About Earl?"

"Yes."

"I guess he had a chance, but he hasn't said anything. We don't talk very easily."

"How come?"

"I don't know," I said. "He seems to be kind of uptight all the time."

"How about you? You a little uptight, too?"

"Could be. Does he talk to you much about it?"

"I'm not much help either," she said. "Adopting a child is so different from what I thought it would be. With your own child you don't have to weigh the pros and cons of having him. There it is, a child. And there are other things involved besides the child, too."

"Like what?"

"Well, from my point of view, I was proud of myself. You know, look what I did—that kind of thing. Then you see it—I saw it—as an act of love—you came from the love I had for your father. The child looks like you—that helps. You see yourself being . . . extended. It's like I can't die as long as you're alive."

"How about that stuff about sharing our home. That's what we were talking about before Earl came."

"I'd still like to share our home, and I'd like to share it with Earl. But once we accept Earl permanently, we accept him as part of our family. Every time he fails or we fail with him, the family fails. I'm not so sure I can handle that."

"Dad's not sure, either."

"I think he's almost sure. It would help if he was positive that it was the right thing for Earl and for you. When you came back from that trip, he seemed to want to go through with it very much. But then he did some more thinking. . . . As soon as you stick your head in it as well as your heart, you have a problem."

"What was that trip all about, anyway?" I asked. "I mean, I liked it and everything, but it was a little off-beat for us, wasn't it?"

"The counselor at the agency suggested it," she said, picking up an avocado. For as long as I can remember, my mother has picked up avocados in the supermarket and has never bought one. "He, the counselor, said that it would be easier to make a decision if we saw Earl

113

away from the home and saw the two of you together in a different—no, neutral—setting. Your father said that the two of you got along just fine."

"Yeah, I guess so."

"What do you think? You want us to adopt Earl?"

"I don't know."

She smiled and turned quickly away, pretending to look at the labels of some canned mushrooms. I stepped around her and looked at her face, and our eyes met and we both smiled.

"How come you're smiling?" I asked.

"It's a hard decision," she said. "It makes us people."

"What does that mean?"

"That we're not machines. None of us. We can't just plug in the facts and come out with nice, neat answers. I think"—she looked at me, and the smile was gone from her face almost without her changing expressions—"that your father will be better off when he realizes that. With people you just hope for the best."

"Just check out your heart and boogie on?"

"Something like that, my man," she said, laughing. "Something like that."

JULY 31st   Twimsy:

A very depressing thing happened today. Two weeks ago—no, maybe five weeks ago—it wouldn't have been depressing, but now it is. We all got these green jackets from the neighborhood rehabilitation center. This center got funded through a government grant, and one of their things was to instill a sense of community in the people around the neighborhood. They hadn't fulfilled that part of their funding operation so what they did was to go out and buy a whole lot of green cotton jackets so that anybody who saw that jacket would know we were from that community. Big deal. The depressing thing about it was when Eileen was saying that it was just another example of an agency doing something that no one cared about just because the funding proposal looked good on paper.

AUGUST 5th   Dear Twimsy:

I got a call at Micheaux House today from my mother saying that her cousin in the Bronx was hurt in some kind of an accident and that she was going to go and see about her. My father was going to take off and take her up there. She said that me and Earl should get some pizza or something and she would fix a regular dinner when she got home. Now when you get a phone call in the middle of the day at Micheaux House you have to tell everybody who it was, what it was about and everything. So what happens is this: the seniors think me and Earl should go home and make sure that the house is clean. I'm not sure why, but I got an idea, so I tell Earl and we take off.

Twimsy, this is my idea. Earl and I are going to make dinner. Now, Earl is pretty smart in a way. He can always think of a way to do something so that if you goof up it won't look so bad. I thought that we should make steak, because that's pretty easy, but he says no, let's make something that's really different, because if we goof it up no one's going to say that we couldn't even make something that's simple. So we went to the supermarket and looked around for something that was different.

They had rabbits in the meat section, but Earl looked at me like I was peculiar or something and said that he didn't eat rabbits. I told him they were like hares and not really rabbits.

"What's the difference between a *what*?"

"A hare."

"Yeah, what's the difference between a hare and a bunny?"

I couldn't tell him so that was the end of that idea. Then I had a great idea.

"Let's get an octopus!" I said.

"A who?"

"An octopus, they got them over here in the frozen fish department."

"You know how to cook an octopus?"

"It's gotta be like cooking a fish, I guess," I said. "Cut it up and fry it."

I don't think Earl liked that idea too tough either, but he said okay and we bought a frozen octopus. It came in a plastic bag, and we got that and two boxes of frozen peas.

When we got home and took the octopus out of the

bag, it was so hard that you couldn't even get next to cutting it, so we decided to let it thaw. BIG MISTAKE!

We put the octopus on the counter and went to watch a little television. We didn't get much of a chance to be home in the daytime so it was really cool. Earl said that when he was in the juvenile hall, all they did all day was watch television. I thought that must have been pretty boring, and I told him so.

"It's okay," he said. "You can just look at television and you don't have to think about nothing. Sometimes I used to be glad just to get out of bed and watch television so I wouldn't, you know, lay up and think about things."

We talked for about an hour or so while we watched television, mostly about what it was like in juvenile hall. It didn't seem so bad to me, but when I said that to Earl, he said he didn't think it was so bad either until he found out about some better things. He said, "Think about that!" Now how can you think about something just because somebody says, "Think about that!"

Then we decided to go out and check on the octopus. Twimsy, this is the absolute truth. Just as we got into the kitchen, the octopus moved. Earl looked at me and I looked at him and we both kind of took a step backwards.

"Hey, man," Earl said, "did that sucker move?"

"It looked like it moved to me," I said.

Then it moved again, one of its arms came down real slow, *I mean real slow.*

"I think it's just unfreezing," Earl said. "Why don't you go check it out?"

"Check it out yourself!" I said.

117

Then we had a conference and decided that it was probably just unfreezing, like Earl said, but it had just started so we were going to leave it alone for a while. Then we went in and watched some more television.

We watched *I Dream of Jeannie*, and then Earl said I should go and check out the octopus again. Only this time he was smiling a little.

"What you smiling about?" I asked.

"I think you're scared of that thing out there," he said.

"You so brave you go check it out," I said.

"C'mon, man," he said, "we ain't scared of no octopus. We'll both go."

So we both went into the kitchen. This time all the arms were down and that sucker was sitting right in the middle of the counter looking dead at us. Right then and there I knew that there was no way we were going to cook that octopus. I didn't even want to touch it. Also, I never knew an octopus had a mouth like a bird, but it does. There was only one thing to do—get rid of it before my parents got home.

"Let's put a bag over its head so it won't be looking at us," Earl said.

That was a good idea, and we mapped out the strategy. We'd get a big plastic garbage bag to throw over it. Then one of us would open the door and the other would scoop up the octopus and take it out to the incinerator.

"You grab him," Earl said. "You the oldest."

"You're supposed to be so tough," I said. "You grab him!"

"I can't," Earl said. "I really can't do it. You got to be the man."

I got the plastic bag, and Earl stood near the door.

"When I say three, I'm going after him," I said, and I wiped my hands on my pants.

"I think his left eye just blinked!" Earl said.

I knew I had to get it over with in a hurry. I took a deep breath, let out a karate scream, and ran after the sucker. I scooped him up in the bag and ran toward the door just as Earl jerked it open. Wham! Right into my father!

"What are you guys doing?" This from Dad at the top of his voice. "What's in the bag?"

Why I said nothing I don't know. But I did know that's not what he wanted to hear. He snatched the bag from me and looked in it. Dude jumped about thirty feet straight up. He dropped the bag and everything. I never knew my father could curse like that. There he was standing in the middle of the hall screaming and cursing. Earl was lying on the floor laughing like he was going to bust his guts at any minute, and my mother, who had just gotten to the top of the stairs, was standing there trying to figure out what this slimy thing lying in front of her door was.

Even after the Kentucky Fried Chicken had been delivered and everything had been explained, my father was still mad.

AUGUST 6th   Twimsy:

One thing that Esther Cruz does that's a little funny is to burn these candles. She has different colored candles in glass containers. Some are green, some are white, some have different layers of color. So it's a slow day, and she decides to go buy some more candles and wants Eileen to go with her. Eileen says it's too hot to go and everybody gives some kind of reason for not wanting to go. But I've been so cooped up in Micheaux House that I really want to go anywhere in the daytime. So I volunteer to go with her.

We get the crosstown bus over to Park Avenue and walk down to 116th Street. About half the people over here are Spanish, and the rest are either Haitian or West Indian. The streets are really crowded, too, but in a different way than on the West Side. On the West Side there are all these guys selling stuff on the street or just standing around, but on Park Avenue everybody is moving. There are a lot of women shopping. They all carry their shopping bags to the market with them. Esther goes into a few places, me with her, even though she's not going to buy anything. She said she was just looking.

The air was really still, and the smells were very distinct. You could pass a small restaurant where they sold fried bananas and you would smell those, and the next store might sell spices and you'd smell them, and the next store would sell fish and you'd smell the fish. None of the stores were air-conditioned so the doors were always open, and sometimes the people inside would call you to come on in and buy something. Some of

120

them knew Esther and would call her.

"Hey! Mrs. Cruz! I got these nice porgies just for you!"

"They fresh?"

"Fresh? He don't even know he caught, he think the tide went out!" The guy was holding up a fish and pointing at him.

"Okay, maybe tomorrow," Esther said.

"Esther! Esther!" A small black woman, about as fat as she was tall, waved at us. "Come buy some of these mangoes, they sweet like you used to be, girl!"

"Can't stand nothing that sweet, Maria."

"Child, you is still something!" the fat woman said. "Who that ugly child creeping in your shadow?"

"He's my bodyguard."

"Come here and eat this mango, boy, before I throw it away!" She took a mango, put it on the counter, and then cut it in half with the biggest knife I had ever seen.

She gave me half the mango and Esther half, and we went on. The mango was ripe and as sweet as she said it was, and Esther laughed at me when the juice ran down my face.

The door of the candle shop was closed, but the shop itself was open. Inside the shop was dark and filled with the scent of burning incense. A small, shriveled-looking man sat behind the counter reading a paper. Esther spoke to him in Spanish, and he nodded. Then he got five candles and put them on the counter. There was an air of seriousness about the whole thing, and I didn't say anything. I didn't even eat any of the mango while

I was in the store, either. Esther paid the guy, and he put the candles in a bag. Then he looked at me and spoke in Spanish.

"I don't speak Spanish," I said.

Esther said something to him in Spanish, and he looked at me and nodded. He was brown-skinned, but his eyes were gray and the black part of one of them, the pupil part, seemed not to be in the center of the eye.

"Do you believe in heaven and hell?" he said to me.

"Yeah."

"And have you made a choice which one you want to go to?"

"Yeah."

Then he sat down and started reading his paper again, and we left. When we got outside, I told Esther that I thought that guy was a little spooky. She said it was okay as long as you only bought holy candles from him.

"But I think," she said, nodding her head, "that if you buy the other kind he is different."

"What other kind?"

"Once a woman did a very bad thing to me," she said. "I had hurt myself in a supermarket, and they paid me a thousand dollars. This woman, she looked so nice, came to me and said that she could contact my mother and let me speak to her. Nobody knew this, but my mother had begged me not to leave Santiago. That's where I'm from, in Cuba.

"I didn't listen to my mother, and I left Santiago anyway, and two months later she died. I felt so bad because I didn't have a chance to say good-bye to her. So when this woman said that to me, I said okay. Then she said it would cost me a thousand dollars because she had to buy some special herbs all the way from China. It was all I had, but I couldn't give up the chance to say good-bye to my mother. So I gave her the money and she told me to come to a place the next night. But when I went there, there was nobody there, and I knew she had put a trick on me. So I told Filion—"

"The guy in the store?"

"Yes, and he gave me special candles to burn for revenge. They don't do anything that wouldn't happen anyway, but they let you know about what happens."

"And what happened?"

"That woman died about three months later," Esther said.

"How did she die?"

"She got hit by one of those new buses, those flexible ones."

"Oh."

Twimsy, the more I know about the seniors the less I know about them. I never saw them before as anything except old people, but the more I get to know them the more I see them as individual people. In a way they're even more individual than I am, mostly because they've lived so much and done so much. You can't take that away from them just because they're old, either.

AUGUST 7th   Twimsy:

I worked in the deli today with Santini, and it didn't work out too well. Now, Santini decided that since it was the first day and all that we'd have something really special—lobster. I'm not really much into lobster, Twimsy, but I can dig where Santini's coming from. At the time it sounded like a good idea.

So here's what happened. Santini and London Brown go around and get all the food. They take it all, except the lobsters, to Micheaux House. The reason for this is that we've got to figure a way to keep our food separate from the store's food. Santini says he's trying to work out an arrangement with the store owner that they would sell our food only in the deli. The store owner likes the idea, but he's a little nervous about it. So Mabel, Patty, and Santini are at Micheaux House making salads and things, and I end up in the store at about ten-thirty all by myself.

"You think you can do something simple?" Santini asked me.

This ticks me off a little because of the way he says it. The truth of the matter is Santini now gets along with Earl better than with anyone else. I say I can handle whatever he has to handle. He says okay and tells me when it gets to be eleven o'clock to put the lobsters in the water. I say okay. He also says to make sure the deli area is nice and clean. Fine.

So I start cleaning the deli area, which isn't too bad already. There's a girl from the store who's working there, and she looks a little foreign, and I ask her where she's from, and she says Crete and asks me if I know

124

where that is. I say yes, even though I'm not too sure, but I thought it had sunk into the sea or something. I didn't tell her that, though.

Nobody goes over to the deli part of this supermarket. In fact, not too many people even come into the supermarket. A lady came over to me and asked me if I had any of those delicious grape leaves that "we" people make so well. I wasn't sure if I was supposed to be offended or not, so I pretended not to hear her.

Okay, here comes the bad part. There's the big burlap bag sitting in the corner, and I know that the lobsters are in there because Santini told me they were. About five minutes to eleven I put on this big pot of water and turn it on, and then I go to the bag with the lobsters in it. Twimsy, the suckers are alive! I have never really dealt seriously with a dead lobster, let alone a live one. And I ain't about murdering no lobsters, so I called Santini. He said to just drop their butts in the pot. Yeah, okay.

But you can't catch them, Twimsy, because the suckers snap at you. But I tricked them, I stuck a stick in the bag and when they caught on to that I pulled them out and threw them in the pot. There were five of them in all, and it took me about a minute apiece to get the first three, and then the last two came at one shot because one lobster was holding on to the other one.

Then the guy who owns the store comes over and tells me that there's a phone call for me. I answer the phone and it's Santini. He wants to know if I got the lobsters in the pot, and I say naturally. Then he says that I should run across the street to Micheaux House and help carry the stuff over to the supermarket.

By the time I get over to Micheaux House and see all the stuff, I realize I'm hungry and suggest that we eat first, but Santini says no. Then me and Patty and Mabel Jackson go back over to the supermarket. When we get over there, the whole place is in an uproar. Some woman is holding her dress up around her waist and screaming, and the owner of the supermarket is down on his hands and knees fishing around under a counter.

Then another woman screams and points, and I look and there's one of the lobsters crawling along the floor. I put down the stuff I was carrying and looked behind the counter, and there were three lobsters crawling around in all.

Just then in comes Santini, carrying nothing, and he sees what's going on and he starts yelling and carrying on, and Mabel says he should shut up before he has a heart attack. Anyway, we get four of the lobsters and Santini throws them back into the pot. Everybody was upset, but Santini said it was great publicity.

"I thought I told you to put the lobsters in the pot!" Santini said.

"I put them in," I said. "They must have crawled out."

"Was the water boiling?" he asked.

"No."

"You put the lobsters in cold water?" He looked at me like I was crazy or something. "You put the lobsters in cold water? You thought that maybe they would wait until the water got hot and then they'd crawl back in?"

Twimsy, what do I know about cooking a lobster? If I had known about cooking them, I don't think I would have thrown nothing live into boiling water.

Anyway, when all the people gathered around, Santini told them what we were doing, about the fast-food place and how we're going to have sandwiches and coffee and things at lunchtime every day, and a few of the women said that it was a good idea, and one of them said that she didn't know how fast the other food was going to be but that the lobsters looked pretty fast running across the floor. Everybody laughed, so she said it again.

AUGUST 8th   Dear Twimsy:

The second day at the deli. I wonder if most people know how many ways there are of making a stupid baloney sandwich. One guy comes in and says he wants his with lettuce, mayonnaise, and tomatoes. The next guy comes in and says he wants his with mayonnaise on one piece of bread and mustard on the other. The next guy wants no mustard, no mayonnaise, nothing, just salt and pepper. The next guy wants it with onion, the next guy wants it with cheese, the next guy wants it with "everything." I asked him what he meant by everything and he said he didn't know because he didn't know what we had. So I made it with everything and he said that wasn't everything. I told him that it was everything we had, but Santini says no, that's not everything. So Santini takes the sandwich back (minus one full bite) takes out one slice of baloney and gives it back to the guy. The guy says okay, *that's* everything, and gives me a dirty look as he leaves. Oh, yeah, another guy comes in and asks for an extra slice of bread on a sandwich. A sandwich has two sides, a top and a bottom. You put one slice on one side and the other slice on the other side. Where you going to put a third slice?

"In the middle," Santini said.

Later he says that's what selling is all about. I can see I'm not cut out to be a salesman. Anyway, not a sandwich salesman.

When things slacked off, I covered the salads and meats and everything and put the sawdust down and started cleaning up. Santini waited on one last customer, and then he helped me with the cleaning. Then London Brown and Earl came over. Now, everybody's supposed to take turns cleaning the deli area. So I figured since Earl and London got there later than they were supposed to they could do the mopping. I didn't like the mopping part because Santini, who seemed to be in charge, wouldn't let you leave until the floor was completely dry. Okay, so I'm half finished sweeping, and Santini tells me to let Earl finish the sweeping, and I could go get the mop and start mopping. I said something about "You got to be kidding!"—something like that. Santini gets mad and he tells everybody to leave and that he would do the cleaning himself. So I left, because I figured I had done my part of the cleaning. After a while London Brown comes in to where I am in the rec room at Micheaux House. I asked him where

Earl was and he said that Earl stayed behind to help Santini.

Earl and Santini come in about a half hour later, and they're laughing and things like they've got some big joke going on, and I get really ticked. No matter what happens, Earl can find a way of coming out on top and making me look bad.

So we sit around and I don't say much. Then Earl gets a call. He has to go someplace for an interview. This person who is in charge of his well-being has to talk to him. So he goes to his office, but first he gets my mom's number from me and calls her and tells her he's going to be late getting home. The guy does everything right. When Earl splits, Santini says he wants to talk to me about something. I don't want to hear a thing he has to say, because I figure he's got some good-doing thing to say about how I should have done this or that.

"So how come you have such a temper?" Santini says to me.

"I don't know what you're talking about," I said. "All I want to do is to be treated fair, that's all."

"And you weren't treated fair?"

"I covered the meats, I covered the salads," I said. "I had half the floor already swept. But you got this thing for Earl, you know. Anything he wants to do is cool. He don't want to mop, he don't have to mop."

"You *have* to mop?" Santini said. "You don't have to mop. But that's not the point. You think I have a special relationship with Earl."

"I didn't say that. I just said I wanted to be treated fair, that's all."

"But I do have a special relationship with Earl,"

Santini said. "Let me tell you a story."

I sat down on this chair he has in his room. The back and bottom are stuffed and the arms are just plain wood. "Go on, man."

"You see, you don't have a lot of patience, but you snouldn't. You're young and you're anxious to get on with your life. I know this, I used to be young myself. Me living longer than you makes me a different kind of person than you are. You live mostly for your dreams— me, I live mostly in my memories. No matter what I say from time to time, that's the way it is. There aren't too many things I can share with you. I can share a sandwich, a joke, maybe, right now a story.

"I remember once I lived in a walk-up over on Moylan Place—that's near the elevated trains. I used to hate that place. I had a grocery store on Amsterdam, and I used to walk home thinking about having to walk up those stairs. I lived on the fourth floor. There were sixteen steps between floors. Eight steps and turn, eight steps and turn. That's the way it was for years. Then I moved over to Broadway. That was when Broadway uptown was losing its reputation as a place for swells. This place had an elevator. But you know, I missed those stairs. That place, those stairs, were a part of my life that I was leaving behind. I can tell you that story, but you haven't invested that much of your life in a place for it to mean that much to you. Not yet—you'll have to live a lot longer before that happens."

"Earl's younger than I am," I said.

"But I know a little about Earl," Santini said. "I know he doesn't have a permanent home. So every place he goes, even if it's just for a day or so, he makes an investment. He invests hope. If I tell him how I felt leaving a place, he'll understand what I mean."

"So that still doesn't mean I should mop the floor if he hasn't done anything," I said.

"No, but sometimes it helps to know not only that life isn't always fair, but why it isn't."

At first I went for it, Twimsy. I sat around thinking how I should understand this and understand that, like Santini said. But then I got to thinking, How come I'm the one that has to understand all the time? It might not be Earl's fault that he's in the circumstances he's in, but it's not my fault if I'm better off, either. He can do the understanding sometimes, too. Maybe while he's mopping the floors.

AUGUST 9th   A hard day, Twimsy. Word had gotten around that we were selling sandwiches and coffees and things, and people started coming in around eleven-thirty and didn't stop until we closed at a quarter to three. It wasn't just people who were working in the neighborhood, either, which is what I thought it would be. Some of the people that came for sandwiches and sodas didn't work at all.

We cleaned up and got back to Micheaux House about four, and some of the seniors suggested that the young people take the rest of the day off. Some of us were so tired that we just wanted to sit where we were. If I never see a buttered roll again, it will be too soon.

Me and Earl started home and stopped for a minute in front of a movie. There was a Kung Fu movie playing there and Earl asked me if I knew any Kung Fu.

"A little," I said. I didn't tell him that most of it came from watching movies.

"I think Kung Fu's a bunch of jive," Earl said. "That's just the way them Chinese and that kind of people be fighting. If you can fight you can kick a guy's romp no matter what he think he know about that stuff."

"If you were boxing me," I said, "and I was using Kung Fu I'd waste you so fast you wouldn't know what was happening. You'd go to punch me, and all of a sudden you'd feel this draft and look down at your chest and wonder how you got that big hole there because I would have snatched your heart out for my trophy room."

We started fooling around, him straight boxing and me going through my Kung Fu bit. The way I figured it, I had to win if he was just using his hands and I was using my hands and feet. We weren't really hitting each other, just bringing our hands close enough to touch the other guy.

"Hey, man," I asked, circling to my right with my hands stiff in front of me like I had seen Bruce Lee do once, "what you think about staying with us?"

"It's okay," he said. He was doing a lot of feinting with his head and trying to get me to drop my guard.

"How come you didn't stay with anyone else before?" I asked. I threw both my hands up, dropped my head, and threw a a sideways kick at him.

132

Earl stopped the sparring and stood looking at me.

"How come you asked?" he said. There was an edge to his voice.

"Just wondered."

"One lady was trying to buy a house," he said. "She saved up the money to get the down payment while I was staying with her. They had like a goal, this big thermometer which they had like you see outside of churches sometimes. Instead of having degrees on it, they had it marked off in so many dollars. Everybody chipped in, and every time they would get to a new amount of money they would mark it off on the calendar, see."

"You helped, too?"

"Yeah, I was doing little things like carrying packages at the supermarket. You carry a package for a lady, she gives you a quarter, maybe fifty cents, sometimes even a whole dollar. Then I put my money up, and they moved, and they thanked me for helping and everything, but, you know, I thought I was going to be moving into the new house."

"That's cold," I said.

"It ain't cold, that's the way it be's. You just make it cold if you go around expecting people to be like television people. Everybody trying to adopt somebody on television. What's that ugly little sucker's name?"

"That Arnold dude on *Diff'rent Strokes*?"

"Yeah. He goes around acting like he supposed to be adopted or something. Then sometimes people want you to act different than you are, they want you to be real smart or something like that—I don't know. I think they right, really."

"I don't think so," I said.

"How come?"

Earl started throwing punches at me again in real slow motion as we talked.

"I don't know how come," I said. "It just doesn't seem right."

"Yes, it do," Earl said. "You think when people be getting a natural kid they ain't got no choice. They got them a choice. They can dig the kid or they can not dig the kid. If they don't dig the kid, then you got somebody like me. Most of them kids that I be with got parents. Their parents just don't dig them, that's all."

"They have white kids there, too?" I asked. The punches Earl was throwing were coming harder and harder, and I started to back off a little.

"They're all kinds," Earl said.

He was punching still harder, and I tried to smile and make believe we were still playing, but it had changed into something else, and his punches were beginning to hurt. I threw a few hard ones at him, too, and I was getting mad. No, Twimsy, I wasn't getting so much mad at him as I didn't want to back down from him. It was like he was saying something to me and not saying something to me at the same time. He wasn't talking at all, just throwing punches, not an all-out fight but fooling-around fighting that was getting harder and harder. It started out as a game, but then we were standing in front of each other and trying to hurt each other real bad, and I don't even know why. I swear I don't even know why, Twimsy.

Finally Earl stopped and just turned and walked away.

There was a big sign that had this white guy holding a glass of wine and looking at this white lady and there was a cat in the background, and Earl leaned against it, kind of half facing it. The guy's head in the sign was a lot bigger than Earl's. Earl looked real little, and I knew he was messed around. Most of the time Earl looked old, or at least older than thirteen, a lot older. But sometimes, when things got to him, and he opened as much as he could open, you could see the kid inside.

I went over and put my arm around him, and he pushed me away gently and walked off. I followed him as we went home without speaking. When we got to the front door, he turned and looked at me. He had the same cool, cocky look that he had had when I first saw him.

"You okay," he said, "you okay."

Twimsy, I felt myself liking Earl again. I asked myself if I liked him or if I didn't like him. It came down like this. He can be two people. One is a kid I kind of like. No, one is a kid I like a lot. The other person is a guy that is either ticked off all the time or doing something that makes him look good while you look bad. This is the part of him I don't like. So I like him and I don't like him. But I want to like him, I really do. Earl is only a nice guy when we're alone. Maybe if he could let the good guy out in public and find out it was okay, we could make it. I don't know.

AUGUST 11th   Jack Lasher got sick today. He was throwing up all over the place, but he wouldn't let them send for a doctor. London Brown said he was always like that.

We got a call from a reporter saying that he had heard that Micheaux House had received some kind of special grant. Eileen told him that she hadn't heard about it, but the guy said he was coming down the next day to interview whoever ran the place.

Somebody told Jack Lasher, and he called a friend that worked on a newspaper so that in case anything bad was written about Micheaux House both sides of the story would get printed. Jack Lasher's friend said that he'd drop by if he could, but he couldn't promise anything.

AUGUST 12th   Twimsy, how do you spell disaster? I spell it R-O-Y-A-L V-I-S-I-G-O-T-H-S!!! First, some background. Twimsy, if anybody at Micheaux House likes us, it's Esther Cruz. Jack Lasher treats everybody fair, but he's really kind of a rough guy. Santini gets on with Earl, mostly, and doesn't seem to like any of the rest of us, especially Patty.

Mabel is a little wary of us, and Eileen is wrapped up in her puzzles and racing forms. You remember how all this got started, Twimsy? How yours truly painted "Royal Visigoths" on a train and got busted? Well, before we got to Micheaux House, they must have told the seniors what we had done, so that's why they figured we were just a bunch of hoodlums and whatnot. But we've been getting along fairly well, and, like I said, Esther likes us. So what she does is to get a friend of hers who still works in the garment center to make up the name "Royal Visigoths" in fancy letters, and then she plans to sew them on our jackets. But when she hears that the newspapers are going to come, she and Mabel Jackson stay up half the night and sew the names on all the jackets, including the seniors' jackets, because Santini said it would be good publicity. So she gets up in the morning and puts out all the jackets so we can have them with our gang names on when we get there, only it's really not our gang name because we don't really have a gang. On the other hand, it's definitely cool.

So we're sitting around when the first reporter comes around, and he's definitely hostile.

He kept asking questions, but whenever anybody answered, he acted like we were lying or something. The seniors were trying to tell him about wanting to keep Micheaux House open, but he said he wanted to know the "real story," what that was. When he left, he said that he'd "find out what's really happening."

Then the guy from the other paper came by, and we told him the same story, and he didn't seem interested at all. He did say that he would try to get a mention of Micheaux House in the paper, maybe on the Only Human page.

Twimsy, today we sold seventy-three sandwiches at

two dollars apiece. Santini says that the profit per sandwich comes to about a dollar ten cents.

"You kidding?" I asked. "That much?"

"Sandwiches are the last illusion of luxury of the poor man," Santini said. "He can walk into a place and demand that another man prepare him a meal. Even though he knows that he can make the same sandwich home cheaper and probably better, he will still come and buy. It's only the poorest who buy sandwiches. The well-off go to the restaurants for the complete ritual."

Santini went on about how the poor have always looked at the sandwich as a step up. He said that when he was a kid the local gangsters in his neighborhood would always send him for a sandwich and give him a big tip. In between customers, we had a sandwich ourselves. I made them, and we were eating them when Hi-Note brought the paper over.

He brought the paper to Santini because he was still a little mad at me. The paper was the one that Jack Lasher's friend worked for.

> HARLEM. A group of local residents have proved that integration works as they band together to clean up their neighborhood. Employing community members of all races, including some troubled youngsters, the Micheaux House Corporation has done a wonderful and spirited job.

"What's this about integration?" I asked.

"What can I tell you?" Santini shrugged. "Some people look at a man and see age, some see color. This guy, a friend of Jack's, sees color."

138

"And troubled youngsters," I added.

"And troubled youngsters."

"It'll still probably be better than the other guy's story," I said. "If he writes one."

Hi-Note left without saying anything else, and I really felt sad when I watched him go.

"Something wrong between you two?" Santini asked.

"Yeah," I said. "Remember when you suggested that I break up that fight by taking Earl's place?"

"He's still mad about that?"

"Yeah, we were pretty good friends," I said.

"You should never abandon a friend," Santini said. "For any reason. That's my philosophy."

"That's *what*?" I couldn't believe my ears. "You were the one that suggested that I get in the argument to begin with!"

"That was my philosophy for *that* side of the fight," Santini said, slicing a tomato. "For this side of the fight I have a different philosophy. How can you have the same philosophy for two different sides?"

AUGUST 13th   Mom told me today that they had started the process to adopt Earl. What a relief! Now that the decision is made, it seems so natural and so right I can't even figure out what all the commotion was about. We went out to eat, not because of a celebration or anything like that, but because Mom destroyed our

139

dinner. She's forever trying out these new recipes that she gets from the *Times*, only she wants to be a little inventive. She gets this chicken and beats up on it or something until you could hardly tell there are any bones in it. I'm watching her the whole time. Then she puts it in this new pot that she bought which really looks like a flowerpot—anyway it's made of the same material that a flowerpot is made of. Then she puts some water on the chicken, some broth mix, and some onions, and sticks it on the stove. Then she looks at the recipe again and this little "Oh!" comes out. What it is, she thought that this chicken was going to be finished in an hour, but it's going to take two hours at least, and she doesn't want to wait that long until supper. So she decides to improvise and cook it in the oven. But she can't even cook it straight that way. She decides to smear honey all over it.

"How come you're doing that?" I asked.

"Makes the skin delicious," she says. She's got this good-doing smile on her face, too.

So she puts this beat-up chicken with honey smeared all over it in the oven and turns the oven on. Everything's cool for a while, and I'm in my room checking out some television cartoons, and she tells me she'll be right back because she's going to the store to get something to make yellow rice.

I'm checking out the cartoons, and all of a sudden I smell this smoke. At first I don't make too much of it, but then there's a knock on the door, and when I go to see who it is, thinking my moms has forgot to take her keys, I see the house is full of smoke.

140

I open the door and it's Earl.

"What you doing, man?" he says, looking in the house over my shoulder.

"Nothing," I said. "Something must be burning."

"No lie?"

It didn't take us long to figure it was coming from the oven. I ran over and turned the oven off. We opened the door and the chicken was all black.

"Now what?" Earl asked.

"I don't know. What do you think?"

"If it ain't a friend of yours, I think we should split," he said.

So we went on into the room and I told him what my mother had done to the chicken. Then my moms came home, and she saw the smoke, and I could hear her running to the oven. There was some scurrying around, and then she came to our room and asked what had happened.

"The stove started smoking and we cut if off," I said.

She looked real pitiful, and we all went out to the kitchen. The chicken was on the counter, one leg pointed up and one leg pointed kind of sideways. Most of it was black, but you could see that it wasn't even cooked on the inside.

"You beat it up like that?" Earl asked.

My mother nodded.

"You beat it up and then you burned it." Earl had this silly look on his face. "You say anything about its mother?"

Mom began to laugh a little, and in a minute we were all laughing together.

We went out to dinner at this real cool Korean place. By this time Mom was pretty much okay, and we got on her a little bit more about the chicken.

"Would you guys like to make supper?" she asked.

"He can make some bad sandwiches," Earl said. "Right?"

"That's right. Salads, too," I said.

We went on like that awhile until the main course came, and then my father started talking about baseball. I knew that he didn't like to stay on my mother's case too long, even if we were just fooling around. So I switched off and Earl did, too, which I was glad of because it meant he was hip to what was going on.

The waitress served the hors d'oeuvres, and Earl gave me a look.

"What's wrong?" my mother asked.

"What are these things?" Earl asked, pushing one of the small meat balls with his fork.

"It's called wanja," my mother said.

"Looks like a hamburger to me," Earl said, a small smile on his face. "All they got to do is to make it a little bigger and flatten it out some."

Earl had wanted, as per usual, a cheeseburger. Mom had said that they didn't serve cheeseburgers but that wanja was close enough for Earl. I could just imagine him thinking about a small piece of cheese to put on top of it.

The supper went fairly smoothly, except for my father, who insisted that he could eat with chopsticks even though most of the food fell back on the plate. That wouldn't have been a big deal either, except that Mom was embarrassed by it. Then, just as we were about to finish the meal, Dad dropped the bombshell.

"Earl, have you given any thought to what name you want to use?" he asked.

"What name?" Earl looked up at him. "You don't like Earl?"

"Earl's just fine," Dad said, "but how about a last name? You'll have to make a decision soon. You can continue to use Goins if you want, or you can switch to Perry."

"Or you can use both names, Earl Goins Perry." Mom smiled.

Earl didn't say anything. He put his head down a little and his jaw moved as if he was trying to chew. Then he swallowed hard.

"Is everything okay?" Mom asked.

It was, Twimsy, only Earl was so choked up he couldn't say anything. He just sat there and looked down at his plate. I just hoped my father knew how Earl felt and wouldn't say anything stupid like "You do want to be adopted, don't you?"

"You do *want* to be adopted, Earl?"

Earl nodded. You think my father let it stop there? Uh-uh. He kept it right on up, and he was really enjoying it. He wasn't doing anything wrong, but he was enjoying how he was making Earl feel. Even though that was good, the way Earl was feeling, it bothered me.

Twimsy, sometimes you can take something that seems so simple, like Dad making Earl feel good by telling him that we, or at least my parents, were going to adopt him, and it ends up not being simple at all.

143

Like that thing with Santini saying he had two philosophies, one for either side. I kind of know what he means, and I don't like it. Things are better when they're simple and what's right is written down somewhere. I guess I'm supposed to want to know both sides so I can make good judgments, but to tell the truth, I can't see where it's always an advantage.

AUGUST 14th   Twimsy:

Good news, bad news. The sandwich concession is working out great! Eileen figured out that we were making a gross of one hundred and twenty-eight dollars a day and a net of seventy-two dollars. We made the biggest gross on the sandwiches, but over half the profit came from the coffee and soft drinks.

"Of course, if we include labor, then we're down considerably," she said. "But if we assume our efficiency will increase and word of mouth will increase our business, we'll do nicely. We should, if my figures are correct, clear two hundred and fifty dollars a week if we can hold up."

"What do you mean *if* we can hold up?" Santini said. "We're doing just fine."

"Would anyone like to check my figures?" Eileen held up a long yellow sheet filled with rows of neat figures.

Hi-Note said that he would check them, and we all got a big kick out of that because Hi-Note couldn't even

144

count to eleven without taking his shoes off. He looked at the figures for a minute and then gave them back to Eileen, saying that they looked all right to him.

The last item on the agenda was finding out how the sandwich business worked without the help of the young people. Santini made a few cracks about who was going to take the lobsters for a walk if we weren't there, but generally speaking, they were pretty sure of themselves, and I was too.

AUGUST 15th   Twimsy:

Dad came in the bathroom while I was brushing my teeth and said something about how big I was getting. Then he asked me if I wanted to hear something silly, so I said okay.

"I love you," he said.

Just like that. He just laid it out. I asked him how come he said that, 'cause he never says things like that.

"Just wanted to say it," he said. "Guess I've been thinking a lot about it."

"More than Earl?" I said it before I even thought about it, Twimsy, I really did.

"Yeah, I know I do," he said. "Does it make a difference?"

You know I didn't know what to say? I just stood there looking at him, and he was there looking at me and looking like me, too, for a long minute. Then he gave me this quick little hug and left. I'm glad Mom didn't come in, she'd have cried or something.

Twimsy: This you won't believe. Santini got arrested! Here's what happened. This woman who worked in the dentist's office on St. Nicholas near the corner of 125th Street had to come to the 116th Street Station to get the A train because the 125th Street Station was closed due to a fire. She's walking down Manhattan Avenue and somebody snatches her purse. The police came and asked her what happened and if she could describe the guy that did it. She said she didn't know what the guy looked like and that there might have been more than one. Somebody shoved her in the back and then she thinks that somebody else grabbed her pocketbook.

A guy on the block said that a bunch of old ladies gathered around, and one of them said that there was a new gang on the block and that she thought that some of them hung out in Micheaux House. Well, the police weren't too interested because lots of people get their purses snatched and the lady didn't actually see anybody anyway. But then who comes down the street all decked out in his Royal Visigoth jacket that his very own Esther Cruz made for him? That's right, Twimsy, Santini!!

So one of the ladies points him out and said that he was a member of the gang. So the police call him over and they see he's kind of old, but what they don't see is that he don't like to be called old or all those cute little names people call seniors.

"Hey, Pop, come over here," this cop said.

"I'm not your father," Santini shoots back. "I'm a very particular man!"

146

The people on the block see that Santini is a senior, too, but they don't want to hear from anything because he's got this jacket on. Even though he's walking with a cane. Right, Twimsy, *the* cane.

The cop thinks he's going to fool around with Santini a little and asks him if he has any dangerous weapons. Santini doesn't like to be played with, as I said, and he pulls out his sword. A woman screamed and the cop jumped back about three feet. He put his hand on his gun, but he didn't actually take it out. The woman whose purse was snatched started mouthing off about how Santini should be ashamed of himself, and before you know it they got Santini in the back of a police car and hauled off to the local precinct.

After he calmed down, they got him to call Micheaux House, and London went over and picked him up.

This all happened last night after we left, and we found out about it in the morning. Only Eileen was in the rec room when we got there, as usual. She rushes out every morning to get her racing form and crossword and starts on that while the others are having breakfast. All she has is black coffee, usually.

We were waiting for Santini, and when we knew he was coming, we had Patty lie on the floor, and we all stood around fanning her. Eileen just watched us and shook her head.

"What happened to her?" Santini came over and peered down at Patty, who had her eyes closed and hands folded on her chest.

"She just found out that we're working in the same house with a juvenile delinquent," Hi-Note said. "Isn't that terrible?"

"Yeah, man." Earl shook his head. "We heard they had to take one guy away in a squad car and everything!"

"So you think that's funny?" Santini's face reddened. "Well, I'll tell you that it's not. They take one look at me and think they can laugh. I know more about life than they forgot!"

"I know what you mean," Hi-Note said, with his eyes as wide as he could get them. "We got busted the same way!"

"Then you shouldn't think it's so funny," Santini said. "When somebody can look at you and insult you because you're old, or because you're young, or because you're black, or because you're . . . you're whatever you are, it's all the same. And what it's not is funny!"

Twimsy, for the rest of the day he stayed in his room. Hey, it was funny, but I guess it wasn't funny. Santini knew a lot of good stuff. Maybe he didn't practice it all, but he knew a lot.

AUGUST 16th   Twimsy.

It's Saturday afternoon right? Me and Earl are home alone trying to figure out how we're going to get out of my father's being ticked off. When we were eating breakfast he came out of his bedroom all dressed. Now, this is unusual, because on Saturday mornings he usually sleeps late. Sunday mornings, too, until my mother starts talking about making afternoon services. Anybody

148

in their right mind would rather get to church early and get it over with rather than miss the ball games in the afternoon. So when he comes out all dressed, I figure something's up. Right-O!

"How would you guys like a treat today?" he says.

Now you just don't jump into a treat with my dad. He can give you a cold and think he's doing you a favor because he's building up your immunity or something.

"What did you have in mind?" I asked.

"The Guggenheim Museum," he said.

"I don't think so, Dad," I said, trying to keep my eyes focused on a sweet and sagey sausage patty. "We're supposed to be playing ball in the park later."

That went over like a stray dog at a flower show. First he humphed a bit, and then he cleared his throat and twisted himself around until the lecture reached the top. He went on about Life not being about basketball, and Life not being about this, and Life not being about that. I should have known better, because art is his thing, and every so often he gets a bug about it. At about two-year intervals, really.

So this goes on until my moms says how much she sure would like to go see the exhibit he's talking about and won't he please take her? Now I know it's not the same taking her because he can't talk to her like he could talk to me and Earl. Like once he took me to see some pictures and I asked him why I should like them. He said I didn't have to and I said that was good because I didn't. Then he got pissed off and said I didn't have any taste. I asked him if I would have had taste if I liked the pictures, and he said that wasn't the point.

So me and Earl are lying there figuring out what to

149

do when they get back so he won't spend the rest of the day on our cases. Earl said we should go to a different museum so when he asked us what we did all day we could lay that on him. That would have blown his whole program, and we were cracking on that when there's a knock on the door. Hey, not a little knock but like the knock of Doom or something.

"Why don't you answer the door, man?" I said.

Earl gave me a look, put on his cocky look, and opened the door.

There was this big dude standing in the doorway. The fool must have had his nose right up against the door because he was halfway in the house when Earl got the door open. He was big and ugly with a nose that filled up most of the middle part of his face.

"Earl Goins and Stephen Perry?" This cat comes up with a big ugly voice to match his big ugly face.

"They don't live here, man," Earl said.

"What's your name?" This guy is in the house, and I'm shaking.

He's got his face about two inches from Earl's.

"Who?" Earl asks.

"I see I got me a couple of clowns," Big and Ugly says. He reaches into his inside coat pocket and pulls out his wallet. But when he reaches in, you could see a holster. He flips open his wallet and there's a badge of some kind, and then he flips it closed again. "I'm Bill Forde."

Now the name rings a bell somehow, but I can't figure out why. He tells us to sit down, and I look at Earl and I see he's ready to run. Then this guy announces that he's our parole officer. He's in charge, he says, of

150

making sure we stay on the straight and narrow.

Then he goes through this whole thing about how we'd better keep straight and what was going to happen to us if we did this or if we did that and how he was taking a personal interest in the case and everything. Then he whips out some papers and tells us to sign the papers so that if we foul up there won't be any mistake about how we were warned. I took a look over at Earl, and my man was sitting there so cool it wasn't funny. He had a toothpick in his mouth, and it just moved from one side of his mouth to the other real cool as if he had everything under control.

Big and Ugly handed me the papers first, but Earl took them and looked them over, and when Big and Ugly asked who he thought he was, taking the papers, Earl just ignored him.

We signed the papers, listened to Big and Ugly talk some more about how we'd better keep ourselves clean, and then we locked the door behind him after he split.

"Man, that dude scared the pee out of me," I said.

"That's what he wanted to do," Earl said. "He ain't no parole officer, he's a youth worker. He should have been here or at least checked with us once a week. Instead he comes around and tries to make it so you're glad he don't come around. That's why we had to sign a couple of times. Each one of them signatures means he's been here."

"Well, he's right about one thing," I said. "I sure don't want to see him again."

"Yeah, but where would he have been if you had needed his butt?"

I couldn't imagine myself ever needing that guy, but

Earl was mad, and I guessed he knew what he was talking about.

We decided to go to the museum, and I thought we should go to the Museum of Natural History, but Earl said no, let's go to the one my father had talked about.

"Then we can say, 'Yeah, we thought about what you said and it sounded good, so we came.' "

I didn't think much of the idea, but I went along because I wanted to ask him something, and I figured if I did what Earl wanted it would be easier. We walked over to Fifth Avenue and got the bus and went to the museum.

For a while we went around acting like highbrows, talking fancy English and stuff like we really knew what we were doing and seeing.

When he's playing around, Earl is so funny you don't think he's the same guy. He even looks younger. What's really strange is that he can be one way one minute and completely different the next. One thing I couldn't imagine him doing was armed robbery, but I had seen it on his record and asked him about it.

"How you find out about that?" he asked.

"When they sent a letter telling about you, they had that in the letter," I said.

"Your parents showed it to you?"

"No, I steamed the letter open."

"No lie?"

"No lie."

"Turkey!"

"You really did an armed robbery?"

"Yeah."

"You don't want to tell me about it?"

"You remember when Jack Lasher said he wasn't proud of killing that guy?"

"You never killed nobody," I said.

"No, but I did the robbery. But now I'm not, you know, proud of it or nothing."

"You do anything else?" I asked. "I mean like armed robbery, stuff like that?"

"Yeah, I did some other stuff, but they didn't catch me for it," he said.

"Like what?"

"You remember all them missing people?"

"What missing people?"

"All of them!"

"There're thousands of missing people."

"Who you think got 'em?"

"Get out of here!"

We roamed around the museum for a while longer and were just about ready to go when who do we see but my parents. They're coming down this hall right toward us, digging on the pictures. Now, the way I figure, my pop must have been really giving Mom the lecture thing because they could have seen the whole museum twice by now if they were walking at a regular rate of speed.

So me and Earl are standing in front of this picture, and I'm talking like my father talks about composition and whatnot, and we're both trying not to crack up when here they come.

Twimsy, guess who blew the scene? That's right. Mom cracked up. I guess she had been hearing the lectures for so long she needed to crack on something.

Dad wasn't sure what was going on, but that didn't stop him from talking about how he was glad we weren't "immune" to a little culture. Mom and Earl walked ahead of us a little, and Mom put her arm around Earl.

AUGUST 17th   Twimsey:

Earl and me get these invitations to dinner at guess where? Micheaux House! Mabel Jackson sends us these invitations to come over for dinner on Sunday afternoon. I say I don't want to go, but I decide to go anyway, because I figure Earl is going to say he wants to go, and go on about how he really cares about the seniors and everything. So I tell my moms about the invitation and say that I'm going. So what does Earl do? He says he's *not* going. He says he's going to call up and say that he's not feeling well and maybe he'd come some other time so that Mabel Jackson doesn't have to put out the money to feed us and everything.

Well, Twimsy, I want to punch Earl out. I figure I can't beat him, but I'd like to get one punch in, just one. Then, dig this, Mom says to me, "I hope you cleaned your room." Naturally I hadn't cleaned it, but Earl jumps right in and says for me to go ahead, he'd clean the room. Off he goes looking like Little Lord Fauntleroy.

Mom walks me to the door, and I'm feeling pretty miserable.

"Don't worry about it," Mom says.

"Worry about what?"

"What Earl has to do to try to make people like him," she says. "As he gets more sure of himself he'll get out of it."

"Yeah, but you seem to dig it," I said.

"I'm glad—your father and I are both glad—that he's trying to get us to like him," she said. "He's trying wrong, but he's trying."

Twimsy, can you dig on that? They've got Earl's whole number! She even knew, I think, that he was going to go clean the room when she said that. If she had a journal like this, I'd give a million dollars to read it.

Okay, so I go to Micheaux House and Mabel has me in her room. She's bought three dinners from the church she goes to. One for me, one for her, and one for Earl. Only Earl, of course, isn't there. So we eat the dinners, and we're talking back and forth, nothing heavy, and then she drops this bombshell on me.

"What's it like being black these days?" she says.

"What?"

"Oh, when I was a girl it was easy," she said. "I bet it's hard now, ain't it?"

My first thought was that she had cracked up. That was my second thought, too.

"I don't know what you're talking about," I said.

"You can go on and tell me, I ain't gonna tell nobody," she said.

"It's okay," I said.

"When I was young, it sure was okay," she said. "Wasn't much you could do or nothing, so if you got yourself straight with the Lord and didn't look no fur-

155

ther than your hands you was okay. You could get by if you put your hand to some work. That's the truth. God knows that's the truth. My granddaddy said when he was born, back in slav'ry times, you did your can to can't till you couldn't do no more, and that was what it was all about. You know about that?"

"Uh-uh."

"You don't. Ain't nobody told you?" She looked at me kind of funny. "What you did was when you got to age you got up as soon as you can see and you be workin' till you can't see. Then you didn't have nothing to worry about.

"Then after that you did what you could, what they let you do, which wasn't that much to worry about neither. Now, you children don't even know nothing. You running around here with them little labels on your backsides and carrying on to beat the band. You so cute and everything it sure is funny. I ain't got a bit a idea how it is to be like you people. Why don't you tell me what it's like."

"I don't know anything to tell, really," I said. "I guess it's okay."

"Be a secret?" she asked.

"No."

"That's all right," Mabel Jackson said. "You just go on and run along. Some things you got to keep to yourself. It's better that way, ain't it?"

"Yes, ma'am."

Twimsy, I couldn't figure if Mabel Jackson was talking sense or not. I saw London down in the day room watching a preseason football game. I told him what happened, about how Mabel was talking and everything. He just told me not to mention it to her again, and that he would look in on her that night. I hope she's all right.

Also, Earl and me were washing dishes Sunday night, and he sees his skin all wrinkled and says something about he wonders why that happens. I told him soap goes through your pores and makes bubbles under your skin. Twimsy, I think he half believed me. Earl's a kid!

AUGUST 18th   Miss Davenport showed up at Micheaux House this morning and said that Michaels, the guy who runs the programs for the aged, is coming by at two o'clock in the afternoon. Everybody sat around and said so what, who cares, stuff like that. But you could see the seniors were all nervous and I guess the nervousness got on to us, too.

"He's either going to think that what we're doing is a great idea," Jack Lasher said, "or he'll think it stinks."

"Then we got to make him think it's a great idea!" Esther Cruz said.

That was just about what everybody felt, Twimsy. The young people cleaned the place up, and the seniors got ready for the sandwich shop. It was decided that they would handle it by themselves so that Michaels would see that they could.

The morning passed so slowly you wouldn't believe

it. When lunchtime came, the young people, one by one, went into the store and checked on the seniors. Everything was A-OK. Finally two o'clock came and Michaels shows up in a limousine. Patty said we should paint "Royal Visigoths" on the side of it, but we vetoed that rather quickly, although it was a cool idea. At three o'clock Jack Lasher came in with the supplies on the wagon he had made out of an old grocery cart. The other seniors followed in a minute, and they were happy. They had done it!

Michaels called a meeting. Before everyone got there, Santini told me that a group of nuns who were visiting Rice High School had come in and ordered about twenty-five sandwiches.

Michaels had Eileen go over the books. He started off by telling her that he had been an accountant for ten years before he began working for the city.

"Well, that shows," she said in this real sarcastic voice, "that nothing is incurable."

He didn't like that one bit, but Eileen didn't care. She went over everything very carefully, and he just sat there nodding his head. When she had finished, he asked her if he could borrow the books for a few days, and Eileen said that he could if he brought them back to her in person and put them personally into her hands. Twimsy, when a senior jumps bad, they jump *bad*.

As soon as Michaels left, the seniors finished telling us how everything had gone, and it was together.

"We've been doing it for a while," Mabel said. "That helped a lot. Then when all them sisters came and ordered their sandwiches it kept the whole place busy for most of the lunch hours. The sisters being there kept the construction workers in line, too."

"One bulky young man with tattoos started giving us a hard time because he thought he ordered rye instead of white," Eileen said. "He was wearing a crucifix, so I asked him why I didn't see him in church Sunday."

"Didn't that shut his butt up?" Mabel clapped her hands. "Only side of the church that fool know is the outside."

We kind of took the rest of the day off while Miss Davenport checked our supplies and told us that she probably couldn't get us much this time.

"Whatever you can get," Eileen said, "would be appreciated by some group. At the moment we don't need it, though."

All of the young people slapped hands on that, and Miss Davenport smiled too. Now all we had to do was to wait until the next week to see what Michaels had to say.

AUGUST 20th   Twimsy—there was a phone call for my father, and he called my mother into the bedroom to talk about it. That meant nothing because if there's anything my father likes it's a would-be secret. Mom was always telling me things that he told her not to tell anyone.

But this time there was something to talk about. What

had happened was this. You have to send in an application for adoption. Then, if your application is approved, you can send in a petition for adoption. Then, if that is approved, you can take the whole thing to court and adopt whoever it was you were after. When Pops sent in the application for adoption, Earl's mother was notified. She wanted to come see the home that Earl was going to stay in, and the person on the phone had called to make an appointment. Saturday morning was going to be the big day.

AUGUST 21st   Twimsy:

Short note today. Everything fine at Micheaux House and at home except for the fact that I received a letter from the public library saying that I owed fifteen dollars for two books I borrowed last winter! I thought sure I had taken those books back, but I found them on my shelf. So I took them back, and the lady in the library says that I have to pay the fifteen dollars anyway.

"How come?" I asked.

"Because the books were replaced," she said. "We didn't have the books because of your negligence in not returning them, we had to replace them because of your negligence in not returning them, now you have to pay for the books because of your negligence."

There's no justice in the world and I have to figure out where I'm going to get fifteen bucks. Maybe I'll take an encyclopedia and hold it for ransom or something. These are desperate times.

August 23rd Twimsy:

I had thought about showing Earl this diary someday, but now I can't. You should have seen his mother! I figured that she was going to be very poor-looking, maybe kind of dark. You know, Santini's always talking about looking at people and seeing something that's in your mind and not what you're seeing? Well, I see people even before I see them, and they look a certain way. If you said to me, "What does a mailman look like?" I don't know what I'd say, but I know I'd *see* in my mind a tall guy who is a real regular-fellow type and smiles a lot. That's a mailman to me. If you ask me what an engineer looks like, I'd say a guy that dresses kind of sloppy, needs a haircut, and is just a little bit under-average in looks. You get the picture? Anyway, I know this is wrong, but that's the way it is. So to make a long story short, I have this picture of Earl's mother being a mousy-looking creature with dark clothes on. So what comes in? Just the opposite. She's a little over average height for a woman, she wears dark glasses and a really sharp dress, and she's got on all these rings and things. And she doesn't talk like a regular person either—more like she's making speeches.

She doesn't look too much like Earl, but you can't

tell a lot with the glasses and she never once took them off. Also, Twimsy, she swallowed a lot. Like, she would stop a sentence right in the middle and swallow, which to me is pretty strange. She seems nice, though, really. I couldn't figure out why Earl would be away from home with a mother like that.

"The only thing I'm interested in," she said, "is Earl's environment. Some people can deal with boys and some can't."

"We don't have a large house," my mother said. "He'd share a room with Steve."

"You're Steve?"

"Yes, ma'am."

"Do you consider yourself a happy child?"

"Yeah."

"Well, that's good," Mrs. Goins said. "Most child psychologists feel that if an older child is happy within the confines of a home, then the younger sibling, or pseudo-sibling, will also be happy."

"We're willing to try very hard to make a good home for Earl," Dad said.

"For both boys," Mom said. "Would you like to see their room?"

Mom shot me a glance, which meant that she sure hoped that we had cleaned the room up well, even though my father said that it wasn't important, that only the general condition of the home was.

"No," Mrs. Goins said, "but I would like to see how the living room looks."

She was smiling, and my mother smiled back, the way you do sometime when someone is smiling and you're not sure why they're smiling. Meanwhile, my man Earl is so nervous I thought he was going to freak out. I can dig it, too. Here he is with two mothers and they're looking each other over and he's right in the middle. When I see him get nervous it makes me a little nervous, too.

Mom takes Mrs. Goins into the living room, Earl is sitting down at the table twisting his fingers, and Dad's turning pages of the newspaper. Mom and Mrs. Goins are in the living room for a pretty long time when all of a sudden I hear what I think is somebody crying. I look at Earl and he didn't hear it, but my father looks up. I go into the living room, and Mom is standing in the middle of the room, and she has an arm around Mrs. Goins, who has her back toward me. Mom motions me away and I go back to the kitchen and get some water. A moment later Mrs. Goins comes into the kitchen with Mom behind her. She seemed okay.

"My, where *did* the time go?" she said. "I have a very important appointment downtown. I really *have* to be going."

"It's certainly nice to . . . to have you drop by," my father said as if he had practiced it in his head first.

"You have a lovely home." Mrs. Goins smiled the same smile. "Why don't you walk me to the station, Earl?"

Earl nodded and got up, and after Mrs. Goins had shaken everybody's hand, including mine, she and Earl left. Soon as they left Mom was crying.

"I feel so sorry for her," she said.

At first I wasn't going to say anything, thinking it was

cooler just to keep quiet, but then I asked how come she felt sorry for Mrs. Goins.

"Because she's a mother and she has to give up her child," Mom said.

"I think she's strange," I said.

"Doesn't make her love Earl any less," she said. "No matter what kind of anger is in her, or what kind of hurt that makes her do things differently, I'm sure she loves him."

"The court decided . . ."

"Even if it's right, it doesn't make it easy," Mom said. "How do you think she must have felt, looking around to see if a strange home is better than her own for her son? She couldn't find the love we have for him, or the care we have for him, and even if she did it wouldn't be her own."

Twimsy, I get the feeling that there are some people in this world who have to spend a lot of their time going around trying to understand the rest of it. Maybe it's your duty to understand if you can. I think what's happening, in a way, is that I know I can understand things if I *want* to. I just don't see any big advantage to it.

When Earl came back he was real down. My folks didn't say anything to him, not even Dad. Earl went to our room and after a while I followed. He was lying on the bed, just looking up at the ceiling, and I sat next to him.

"You okay?" I asked.

"Yeah."

"You want to talk about it?"

"Uh-uh."

164

"How come?"

"What you know to talk about?" he said. "You don't know nothing."

"You can tell me, can't you?" I said. "That's what brothers are for."

"We ain't brothers yet," he said.

"We are if you want to be. You know, whatever happens . . . happens, but we're brothers if you want to be."

"We going to cut each other and mix the blood or something?" He looked at me, smiling.

"Maybe we could just mix some Coke or something," I said. "I'm not really into a whole lot of bleeding. Unless you really want to do it."

"We get some Coke later," he said.

"That's cool," I said. "Hey, look, man, your moms is all right!"

"No, she ain't," Earl said. "Two times before I got somebody that wanted to take out papers on me and she said no."

"She said you couldn't be adopted?"

"Yeah."

"Can she do that?"

"Am I adopted?"

"How is she other than that?" I asked. "I mean . . . you know."

He didn't say anything, just turned away.

AUGUST 26th   Dear Twimsy:

We get to Micheaux House today and all the seniors are fluttering around something crazy and you know something is up. Even Eileen is walking around looking a little daffy. So when we all get there, they ask us to gather around. Eileen says that Santini has an announcement to make.

"Yesterday me and Esther took our blood tests," he said.

I was just about to say something like I guess they came out okay when Patty starts carrying on and screaming.

"So what happened with the tests?" Hi-Note asked.

"You silly duck!" Eileen slapped Hi-Note's arm. "They're getting married!"

Well, that was it. They're getting married. Santini says it was better than living in sin, but the way I figured, he didn't mind living in a little sin, but Esther didn't dig it too tough. Anyway, they said that it would be a lot harder because they would lose benefits, but that they were getting married Thursday.

"How come so soon?" Patty asked.

"At my age," Santini said, "it's never soon enough."

"He just can't keep his hands off me," Esther said happily. "You know how men are. So I thought I'd better make it legal before he gets too nervous."

AUGUST 27th   Earl sprained his thumb really bad. You won't believe how he did it, either. There's this rickety old exercise room at Micheaux House that's worth about two cents. The only thing that's really standing firm are these bars that the seniors are supposed to walk between for exercise if they have leg problems. We use them to do dips on. You put one hand on each bar, pull your knees up, and then dip down to the floor. We had a contest once to see who could do the most, and Patty won, probably because she's the lightest. So the guys go in when Patty isn't around and practice so that we can challenge her again. Earl's on the bars—they call it a stationary walker—and he's doing a handstand. Then he says he's going to flip over the side and dismount like they do on television at the big gymnastics meets. We're just talking about how it ain't a big thing, because the bars are only four feet high, when he flips over and gets his thumb caught in his pocket and almost tears it off. I thought he was going to cry but he didn't. Nothing breaks this cat down.

I'm still thinking about taking out the parts in this journal about Earl's mother and maybe the parts about him being afraid of the dark, that sort of thing, and showing them to him. I'll see how things work out.

AUGUST 28th   Bad news. That Michaels guy comes over with Miss Davenport and another guy. You didn't have to wait to hear it was bad news because you could see that Miss Davenport was upset. The seniors don't even ask what's up, they just wait. Michaels clears his throat a couple of times and then lets it out.

"We've been reviewing the situation here at Micheaux House," he says, twisting a pencil so that he bounces the point on the table and then the eraser alternately, "and we find that it's an intolerable situation. The publicity that the place has received has just served to clarify the issue in our minds."

"How's that?" Eileen said. "It's obvious that you aren't going to say anything that we want to hear, so I think the only decent thing you can do is to at least give us specific reasons for your decisions."

"There have been a lot of stories in the papers—"

"Two," Eileen said.

"Two stories in the papers about Micheaux House. That's two stories too many. All media contacts with city-run agencies or institutions are supposed to go through the city's public relations office. Which means additional costs to the city because there are additional places to cover."

"We're not asking you to run this place," Santini said. "We'll run it ourselves."

"You can't run it yourselves," Michaels said.

"But apparently we can," Eileen said. "Or did the accountants find something wrong with the books?"

"No, the books were in fine order. But the city's attorneys feel, and rightfully so, that if you're operating a business that is in any way conducted on city property, with the sanction of the city, then the city has liability. You're operating a food business, which means that the

168

city is liable for any possible damages, any claims or lawsuits."

"Oh, nonsense."

"Not nonsense at all," Michaels said. "The building will be shut down at the close of business next Friday. In the interim no business other than that initiated by the city will take place here, nor will anybody conduct business who resides here. This is Mr. Schenk, an attorney for the city corporation. If you have any legal questions you can address them to him. I'm sorry, but that's the way it is."

"You're not sorry, Mr. Michaels," Miss Davenport said. "Because if you were sorry you'd be out trying to do something instead of looking for a law to hide behind!"

"Miss Davenport I don't think it proper for you to—"

"Mr. Michaels, go to hell!"

Twimsy:

It was so quiet that you could almost hear it being quiet. Things were past being sad. Being sad means something bad is happening to you, like you're lonely, or something like that. Then you feel bad and that's a kind of sad. But you can hope something good is going to happen. When you don't have anything to hope for, whenever you see the same thing in front of you, or maybe worse, it's different. You don't feel a real good reason for doing whatever you're supposed to do next. It's bad news, Twimsy.

AUGUST 29th   Twimsy:

Santini and Esther got married. When Michaels said the place was going to close, Esther said that they couldn't get married because then they would have to wait for a spot for a married couple in the new place, but Santini said he wouldn't wait. He said he was going to get married even if he had to live in the park. I think what happened was that at first it was Esther who really wanted to get married and Santini was a little shy about it, but once he made the commitment he went all the way.

So they had the wedding at Micheaux House, and Miss Davenport and a lot of people from the neighborhood came. Michaels came, too, but I couldn't guess who invited him. He said something about trying to find a spot for them in the new place right away, and Miss Davenport said that if he didn't she would personally strangle him.

"How come we don't go to the newspapers and tell them what's happening?" I asked Miss Davenport just before the ceremony.

"The better the job the seniors do," Miss Davenport said, "the harder it will be for the bureaucracies-that-be to cope with it. They can't cope with what the seniors were doing. There's no place in the paperwork for individual effort and determination. In this case, better is worse."

Twimsy, the minister was young enough to be the son of Santini and Esther Cruz. But the ceremony was really nice. Eileen played the Wedding March on the piano, and everybody was crying, and Esther really looked sharp. She had on this dress that was just a regular white dress but with a little lace skirt thing that you tied around the waist and a lace shawl that buttoned onto the sleeves it looked just like a wedding dress. Out-of-sight, and she made it herself.

My man Santini was dressed down and was so nervous that Eileen had to hold up the Wedding March while he went to the bathroom.

I wondered about a ring, but Patty said the seniors had all kinds of rings and things.

So they got married, and Santini kissed Mrs. Santini, and we had a party. It was kind of a good party, but everyone knew that Micheaux House was closing, and when people were hugging each other and kissing each other it was for Esther and Santini, like they said, but it was more, too. It was for the closing of Micheaux House and because everybody needed some hugging and kissing in a bad way.

Twimsy, when Santini and Esther got married it was really natural. It was like two people, not two seniors, not two old people, but just two people getting married. I look at the seniors now and I see Esther Cruz and Mabel Jackson and Eileen and Jack Lasher. What I see is people.

I think it started with Earl's mother. I had an image of her, how she would be and all before she came over, but when I saw her I saw just a regular person who has lived a lot different than I have. Okay, so you figure that I see Earl okay, too. But with him I'm still not one hundred percent sure. When he said he actually did that armed robbery I was really shocked. I thought he was going to say it was a mistake or something. He made me mad at him for a moment by not being what I wanted him to be. It didn't last long, but it was there for a moment just the same. That might be important to remember.

SEPTEMBER 2nd Twimsy:

We got a letter from the judge about Earl. My parents had to fill out a whole new set of papers. Earl's mother wouldn't allow us to adopt him, but the court gave my parents custody of Earl until he turned eighteen, then he could make up his own mind.

We went down to see the judge, and he said that it was a fairly common thing. People feel that giving a child up for adoption means that they've failed, but if they only give up custody, it doesn't look too bad.

"Does that mean that she might want to reclaim Earl in the future?" Dad asked.

"It's a possibility," the judge said. He was a big red-faced man with absolutely white hair. "But it's not even nearly a probability. Usually, unless there was a lot of contact before the custody agreement, and in this case there wasn't, there's little subsequent contact."

"But can't she see that adoption could be better for Earl?" my mother asked.

"If she could see things from the boy's viewpoint, this whole discussion would probably be academic," the judge said, going through his papers. "Shall I proceed with the process?"

"Yes." This from my father.

"Mr. and Mrs. Perry, Richard and Jessica, do you both understand the moral and legal obligations of child custody?"

"I think we do," my father said.

"Mrs. Perry?"

"Yes, Your Honor."

"And do you both agree to assume custodial care for Earl Goins and to fulfill those obligations?"

"I do," my father said.

"I do," my mother repeated.

"Will you sign here, please."

My parents signed the papers to take custody of Earl.

"Earl, you're quite a young man now," the judge continued. "Is this what you want—to be in the care and the home of Mr. and Mrs. Perry?"

Earl opened his mouth to speak, and the tears filled his eyes and he couldn't talk. The tears were running down his face, making a mark where his skin was ashy, and his chest was heaving with sobs. He reached out and put his hand on my mother's.

"I'll take the gesture for affirmation," the judge said, "and by the power vested in me by the state and county, declare the custody as legal and binding."

SEPTEMBER 9th   Twimsy:

Started school today. Earl is a grade behind what he should be, but I think he can make it up if he works hard. Maybe. I decided not to show this journal to anyone. I think I want to go over it again and maybe think about some of the things in it some more. Also, I like writing down what I feel. It makes my feelings clearer somehow. It gets my feelings closer to what I'm thinking. Maybe if I showed it to someone else I would be thinking about what they were going to say or think about it and that would change the whole thing. Probably it would.

Eileen never went to the new place. She went to Kansas instead, where she has a brother. He is a retired senior, and what he does is to take smart kids around to dig for fossils and things like that. Eileen wrote a letter telling how her brother's place was so large and everything but that it needed a lot of work. She said if all the seniors at Micheaux House came out, they could fix the place up just fine. She got her brother to write each of the seniors a letter, asking them if they would come.

It sounded like a good idea, Twimsy, but I wasn't surprised that none of them went. Me and Patty and Earl went to LaGuardia House, where Mabel Jackson just about summed it up.

"It could be very good," she said, "but the city, the old neighborhood, that's what I'm all about. I don't have the job I had when I was young, I don't have the health. How much can I give up and still be human?"

Mabel Jackson didn't look too good, Twimsy. There was something in her eyes that made her seem to be

174

looking at us from further away than before. Mabel held my hand the whole time I was there and kept telling me to take care of myself, and I said I would. She said that London Brown came around to see her sometimes, and that she appreciated it. I got the feeling that she was saying that it would be all right for me and Earl to come around sometime, too.

Mr. and Mrs. Santini got an apartment near Park Avenue, and Earl and I went to visit them soon after we had seen Mabel. The apartment wasn't much. The linoleum on the floor was buckled and half the pattern was gone from wear. The sink was one of the old kinds, that looked as if it didn't really belong in an apartment, maybe in a warehouse or something. Esther talked a little about how hard it was to make it from day to day, but she seemed okay. You got the feeling that they were happy together and would be happy no matter how hard it got. They kept making little jokes with each other, and even as Earl and I were going down the stairs we could hear Esther laughing.

We asked about Jack Lasher, and Santini said that he heard that he had gone to live with his son. Twimsy, I saw him about two days ago over on Amsterdam Avenue. His clothes were dirty, and even though it was cool he wasn't wearing a jacket. He had a suitcase with him. I went up to him and said hello, and he nodded and walked past me. I called after him and asked him if he was okay. He stopped, looked back, and said that he was. When I got home I called Miss Davenport at the new place where the seniors were. I told her about seeing Mr. Lasher, and she said that she knew, but there was nothing she could do about it.

"Human beings choose the way they want to live," she said.

She said she was sorry, too. So was I.

You know, Twimsy, the funny thing is that, after writing everything down over the summer and figuring out that there are a lot of things I don't understand, I'm still not sure that I *want* to understand them. Maybe when I get older, and if I get into a position to do something about things when I can understand them, it'll be easier. Another thing that bothers me, something I picked up from being at Micheaux House, is that it's just about impossible to live in this world without some kind of understanding. I mean, one day I'll be a senior like Santini and Eileen and them, and I wonder how I'll be. If it depends on how everybody else treats me, how they understand what I'm going through and everything, it could be shaky. I guess I won't know till I get there.

One thing I *think* I've got straight is me and Earl. Most of the summer I was concerned about figuring him out. But when the final decisions were made, it wasn't him that I had a handle on, it was me.

I still only know a part of what it's like being Earl, and nothing about what it's like being a person like his mother with her dark glasses and her strange smile. Maybe it's not important that I do.

On the other hand if I don't try to understand these things, then what? Who does figure it out or make things better? Guess I'll just continue to write to you, Twimsy, and hope things get a little clearer. That'd really be cool.

Walter Dean Myers is the author of many highly acclaimed books for children and young adults, including the Newbery Honor Book *Scorpions*. Many of his books have been ALA Notable Children's Books and ALA Notable Best Books for Young Adults. He has won the Coretta Scott King Award for four books, including NOW IS YOUR TIME! *The African-American Struggle for Freedom*. Walter Dean Myers lives in Jersey City, New Jersey.